The kiss made Natasha's legs feel weak. She kept telling herself, you're *acting*, Natasha. And so is he.

And still the kiss went on.

Mark looked up from the script. "Too long!" he said. Ashley stopped the kiss and glared across at Mark.

"What did you say?" he fumed.

"The kiss was too long. You don't spend that long doing it with Becky."

"I don't want you directing me, thank you!" yelled Ashley. "I just want you to follow the book and make sure I get the lines right!"

Mark stood and threw the script to the floor.

"Follow your own bloody book!" he said as he stormed out of the room.

Look out for:

Last Summer, First Love:
A Time to Love
Goodbye to Love
Jennifer Baker

Summer Sizzlers
Various

Two-Timer
Lorna Read

Russian Nights
Robyn Turner

Point Romance

Spotlight on Love

Denise Colby

Cover illustration by Derek Brazell

■SCHOLASTIC

Scholastic Children's Books
Scholastic Publications Ltd,
7–9 Pratt Street, London NW1 0AE, UK

Scholastic Inc.,
555 Broadway, New York, NY 10012-3999, USA

Scholastic Canada Ltd,
123 Newkirk Road, Richmond Hill,
Ontario, Canada L4C 3G5

Ashton Scholastic Pty Ltd,
P O Box 579, Gosford, New South Wales,
Australia

Ashton Scholastic Ltd,
Private Bag 94407, Greenmount, Auckland,
New Zealand

First published by Scholastic Publications Ltd, 1995

Copyright © Denise Colby, 1995
Cover artwork © Derek Brazell, 1995

ISBN 0 590 55791 2

Typeset by TW Typesetting, Midsomer Norton, Avon
Printed by Cox & Wyman Ltd, Reading, Berks.

For DENIS BOND

1

Natasha eyed the competition: five equally attractive actresses, all vying for the same part in Coy Productions' sure-fire hit musical, *A Stranger Love*.

As they sat in the green room of the theatre, awaiting the stage manager's call, they flicked through copies of the script, each wondering how they could deliver the lines in an interesting enough way to secure the part.

One of the girls leaned back in her chair and sighed, "She's been gone for ages. What's she doing that's so special?"

The other actresses mumbled in agreement. One of the auditionees had been called some fifteen minutes earlier and still hadn't returned. Everyone was sure that she must have been given the job.

"Surely they wouldn't keep us waiting if the job has already been offered?" asked Natasha.

Her five competitors grinned. This young girl

had obviously just joined the acting profession and hadn't been to many major auditions before.

"Oh, they'll see us eventually," one of them informed her kindly. "But it doesn't mean to say they haven't already cast the part."

"They're probably just looking for the *understudy* now," added another.

The first actress grimaced. She didn't want to be an understudy. She could think of nothing worse than sitting in a theatre dressing-room night after night, waiting for the moment when the actress she was "covering" would suddenly fall ill.

"I'd hate to be an understudy," she said.

"Me too," agreed another of the auditionees, "but there's not a lot of work around, so if it's offered, I'd take it."

"I'd jump at the chance," said Natasha, enthusiastically. "I'd love *any* job in the theatre." She suddenly rethought her statement. Any job but that of an Assistant Stage Manager, she mused, remembering how bad she was as an ASM in her drama school productions.

The stage manager appeared at the door.

"Natasha Ward?" he called.

Natasha stood, straightened her skirt and ran her fingers through her long, blonde hair.

"Yes."

He smiled at her. "This way, darling."

He led her from the green room, down the staircase, passing all the dressing-rooms and into the prop-filled wings at the side of the stage.

Natasha watched the actress still being

auditioned. She was standing by the piano, centre-stage, belting out the title song from the show, *A Stranger Love*.

Natasha whispered to the stage manager, "She's very good."

He winked at her. "Yes. But not right for the part."

"Really?" Natasha suddenly grew confident. "Why?"

"Too plain. Talented, but unattractive." He shrugged. "But then, the casting's nothing to do with me."

The talented but unattractive actress finished her number and a voice from the theatre stalls called, "Thank you! Very nice. We'll let your agent know this afternoon."

"Thanks," she called back. She left the spotlight, walking into the wings ... and almost into Natasha.

"Good luck," she said, automatically.

"Thanks," replied Natasha.

The voice called, "Next!"

The stage manager led Natasha on to the stage and announced, "Natasha Ward."

Natasha was blinded by the lights and couldn't see anything beyond the front of the fore-stage.

"Did you look at the part?" asked a disembodied voice from the darkness of the auditorium.

Natasha gulped. Her hands shook nervously as she held up the script that she was clutching tightly.

"Yes."

The stage manager picked up another copy of

the script, which was lying on top of the piano, and opened it.

The voice called from the darkness. "Our stage manager will read the part of Jonathan ... and you can read Sarah."

"Page fifteen," the stage manager informed Natasha.

She opened the script and began to read.

Natasha had practised this sort of thing so many times at drama school. "Audition technique" was what the college principal had called it. It was never easy to stand up in front of your peers and read a speech from a play, but it had never been as nerve-racking as this.

She read the part of Sarah.

She read it very well.

"Well done!" called the voice. "Come and sit on the front of the stage, Natasha."

Natasha walked towards the darkness and sat with her feet dangling into the pit.

The voice approached and Natasha saw the director for the first time.

Bill Grant was in his early thirties, good-looking with cropped blond hair and tiny round spectacles covering his large blue eyes.

"That was extremely well read, Natasha," he said.

"Thank you," she beamed at him.

"And I believe you've only just left drama school."

"Yes."

"I don't suppose you've read the book, have you?" he asked.

Natasha had been awake until three o'clock that

4

morning, finishing the novel of *A Stranger Love*. It was hard going. Not the usual type of blockbuster. This one had many complicated passages, but if an actress was to truly understand the part of Sarah, then the novel had to be studied from cover to cover.

"Yes. Of course I've read it," she replied enthusiastically.

"Well … very well done," he said again.

"Yeah! Great!" called another voice from a distance.

"This is the star of the show," said Bill Grant, as a tall, handsome and very well-built youth loomed from the darkness.

Natasha almost dropped her script. Ashley Gibson, the heart-throb star of the Australian soap *Outback*, stretched out his hand.

"G'day," he said, smiling, showing whiter-than-white teeth through a perfectly-shaped mouth. He flicked back the black hair which had flopped across his tanned forehead, and his dark brown eyes sparkled as he gripped Natasha's hand.

"Ashley Gibson," he introduced himself.

Natasha wondered if it were cool to be cool! She wasn't sure if she should show that she recognized him from the television.

Director Bill solved her problem. "I expect you've seen Ashley in *Outback*, haven't you?"

"Yes," she stammered, thinking, I never missed an episode until he left the programme. After he'd gone, it wasn't worth watching.

Ashley squeezed her hand.

"How old are you, Natasha?" he asked.

"Seventeen," she replied.

He looked at the director and winked. "Perfect."

Ashley was a mere nineteen, but had been the pin-up idol of millions since his first appearance in *Outback*, when he was just sixteen. Natasha, in those days, had even pinned his picture to her bedroom wall and he'd often appeared in her dreams. She could hardly believe he was standing in front of her now, still gripping her sweating palm in his thick, manly hand.

"We'd like to hear you sing, Natasha," said Bill. "Can you read a score?"

"Yes," she replied.

Ashley released his grip and Natasha leapt up and walked towards the piano.

The musical director, seated at the keyboard, handed her a book of sheet music opened at the number, *A Stranger Love*.

"It's not easy, darling," he warned her. "It covers quite a range."

Natasha cleared her throat as the intro started.

And then she pitched, perfectly, into the opening lines,

Aching hearts are breaking; caring
  For nothing around me, while I'm sharing
A stranger's love.

The musical director smiled approvingly at her. She was definitely better than the last auditionee. And far prettier.

Natasha was stopped by Bill Grant's voice, before she'd completed the number.

"Thank you, darling. We've heard enough," he called. "Very good. We'll call your agent and let him know, sometime this afternoon."

Natasha capped her eyes with her hands, trying to peer through the darkness at the director and to get one final look at the stunningly handsome face of Ashley Gibson. She could see nothing.

"Thank you, Mr Grant," she replied.

As she turned to follow the stage manager from the stage she heard Ashley's voice call after her, "Brilliant, Natasha!"

Natasha sat by the phone, waiting for her agent to ring. He called just after four o'clock.

"Natasha?"

"Yes, Barry?"

"Understudy's yours!" he said. "Interested?"

She gasped. "I don't believe it."

"Money's not very good, but for your first job…"

"I'll manage," she interrupted him. "When do I start?"

"The cast are rehearsing from this Monday," he informed her, "but the understudies aren't needed until Monday week."

"Fantastic!"

"Little problem, though, darling," he went on. "The job involves a bit of ASM work."

"Oh!" She plunged into despair.

"That worries you, does it?" he enquired, sympathetically.

"A bit, yes. Stage Management isn't really my forte, Barry."

"It won't be much, darling, I'm sure," her agent

tried to convince her. "It'll only involve setting a few of the actors' props."

"But I can never remember where anything goes," she groaned. "I was so bad at it at drama school. I failed on the ASM side of the course. I'm terrible."

He was silent.

"I don't want to ASM, Barry," she said. "Really. I'd be absolutely terrified of it."

"I understand," he said, sounding a little disappointed.

"Do you mind?" she asked. "I know it means you'll miss out on your commission, but..."

"Natasha," he assured her, "I don't want you to do anything you're not sure about. Anyway, I've put your name forward for a small television part, so perhaps it would be best to wait."

"Thanks, Barry," she said.

"I'll call Bill Grant now and tell him," he concluded.

Natasha had just helped her mother to wash up the dinner things, when the phone went again. Her father called from the hall, "Natasha, it's for you!"

She hurried to the phone, wondering if it was one of her ex-drama school friends, calling to see how she'd got on at the casting.

"Natasha, it's Ashley," said the voice. "I hope you don't mind me ringing you at home."

Natasha felt her mouth go dry. If she hadn't recognized the voice she would have suspected it was one of her friends playing silly games. But there was no mistaking that deep, warm Australian accent.

"Ashley?"

"Ashley Gibson."

"Yes?" she said, quizzically.

"Is it all right to talk?" he asked. "I got your number from your c.v."

"Yes." She could hardly speak.

"You've turned down the job," he said.

"Yes. I'm … I'm sorry," she stuttered. "I didn't want to ASM."

"I'm sure," he said, sounding sympathetic. "But it's a great shame. You're perfect for the part."

"But I haven't been offered the part," she replied softly. "And if I take the understudy, there's no guarantee that that'll I'll ever play it."

He whispered almost confidentially into the receiver. "Just between you and me, the part of Sarah was already cast. It's being played by Becky Masters. We haven't let the press know yet, because she hasn't actually put her name on the dotted line, but…"

"Becky Masters?" gasped Natasha. She had no doubt that Becky Masters was a great actress and she was certainly extremely beautiful, but Natasha would never have thought that she could sing.

"Yes," affirmed Ashley. "Because of her TV sit-com, she's a big name, Natasha. Becky Masters will certainly draw people in to see the show. And – " he added, " – she's got a surprisingly powerful voice."

"I'm pleased to hear it," said Natasha, "but I still don't want to ASM."

"Natasha," he pleaded. "Think about it. You're absolutely perfect for the role and I'm sure that Becky Masters will never complete the run. From what I hear, she's only got to get a sniffle of a cold and she'll call in sick. And then the understudy goes on! That's why we've got to have a top-class cover, Natasha. That's why we've got to have you."

Natasha realized that she was being cleverly seduced by the Australian heart-throb into accepting the job. She wondered if it were true. Was Becky Masters likely to fall ill? Would the understudy suddenly take over the lead part?

"I'm not sure," she said. "Really. I'm very flattered that you're so interested in me, but..."

"Think about it, Natasha," he insisted. "Don't jump to any decision now. Think about it overnight and I'll call you again tomorrow. All right?"

"All right," she replied. "I'll think about it."

"I've put a lot of my own money into *A Stranger Love*," he confided in her. "And I'm sure it'll be a big success, Natasha. But it's got to have all the best people involved."

She was silent.

"And you've got real talent," he said. "Certainly far better than anyone else we've auditioned."

"Thanks."

"So think about it, eh, Natasha?"

"I'll think about it," she assured him.

He hung up.

"Who was that?" asked her mother as she emerged from the kitchen, holding a damp tea-towel.

"Ashley Gibson," replied Natasha, nonchalantly. "You remember. That boy from *Outback* that I used to go mad on."

"Oh sure," laughed her mother. "Pull the other one. It's got bells on!"

"Well, what do *you* think, Barry?" asked Natasha.

Her agent sounded a little irritated. "I think he shouldn't have called you at home. That's what I think. It's most unprofessional."

"But should I do it?" There was excitement in her voice.

He chuckled. "It sounds as though Ashley Gibson's already persuaded you."

"Do you think I'd ever get to play the part?" she asked.

"That depends on the actress you're understudying, darling," he said. "I don't think they've cast it yet."

"They have," she said, immediately. "But it's still secret."

"Well you'd better tell me who it is," he advised, "because that'll definitely affect my judgement."

She paused momentarily, wondering if she should tell him. "It's Becky Masters," she blurted out.

"No! I don't believe it!" He laughed, heartily.

"What's so funny?" she asked.

"Take it!" he said, firmly. "I used to represent her. She was a client of mine for two years."

Natasha was very surprised. "Really?"

"She's the most neurotic actress I've ever come across," he added. "And she's always ill. She's

11

talented but totally unreliable. Whoever under-studies that part will play it, you can count on that! She'll never last the run."

That's just what Natasha wanted to hear. If she did get to play the part of Sarah, it would be a job made in Heaven. A wonderful beginning to her career. And if, as appeared possible, she could get closer to Ashley Gibson, that man of her dreams ... it could be a *romance* made in Heaven!

"Tell them I accept, Barry," she giggled. "Tell them I look forward to seeing them a week on Monday."

2

Natasha arrived early at the draughty
rehearsal room off Holborn Circus. A plain-
looking lad, about her own age, greeted her.

"There's no one here yet," he said, nervously. "I
made myself some coffee. Is that all right?"

She grinned. "I don't know. It's my first day."

"Mine too." He breathed a sigh of relief. "I
thought you might be someone important."

She laughed.

He blushed. "Sorry ... I didn't mean..."

"Don't worry," she replied. "I'm *not* important.
I'm Becky Masters' understudy."

"Oh! Good," he rushed on, almost tripping over
his words. "I'm Ashley Gibson's understudy. I'm
covering the part of Jonathan." He put out his
hand. "Mark Fallon."

"Natasha Ward," she told him.

She eyed him up and down. He was about the
same height as the delicious Ashley Gibson, but
nowhere near as attractive. He didn't have

Ashley's smouldering dark eyes, nor his tan, nor that jet-black hair.

He noted her quizzical expression.

He shrugged. "I hope I don't ever have to play the part. The audience'll walk out if they see me standing up there."

"Nonsense," she replied, kindly. "I'm sure you'll be very good."

"Would you like a coffee?" he asked, relieved that she hadn't put him down. "There's a tray over there in the corner and the kettle's warm."

She crossed to the tray of coffee cups. "Yes, I would."

He followed her and watched as she put some coffee into a mug. "I can see why they chose you," he said, softly.

"Really? Why?"

"You're very beautiful," he said. "Just as good looking as Becky Masters."

She smiled at him. "Thank you. But I don't suppose I'm as talented as her."

He paused until she'd finished making her coffee. They both sat, silently, on two of the many metal-framed chairs lining the walls of the rehearsal room.

"Are you nervous?" he asked, finally.

"Yes," she said. "A bit. You?"

"Terrified," he admitted. "I was sick this morning, before I left home. It's my first job. I've only just left drama school."

"Me too," she confessed. "My first job too, I mean. I don't mean I was sick."

"But you are nervous?"

"Of course."

The door burst open and Ashley Gibson entered, with a big grin.

"G'day folks," he shouted across the rehearsal room. "You're nice and early."

Natasha couldn't help but notice how beautiful he was. She felt a tingle run up her spine. Even at this early hour in the morning, he was groomed to perfection; looking every inch a star.

He crossed to the coffee corner.

"Mine's black, no sugar," he said to Mark.

Mark stood and began to make coffee for his principal.

Ashley took over his seat and immediately turned his attention to Natasha.

"I'm glad you decided to accept the offer," he said, his warm smile making her feel so important. "I'd've hated it if they'd cast someone with less talent."

"Thanks," she said demurely.

"Or less beautiful," he added.

She giggled.

"Not that I'll get to play with you that much," he grinned, "if you know what I mean?" He laughed. "Unless Becky Masters breaks an ankle."

"I hope not," said Natasha, wide-eyed and mock-concerned.

"She's very good, mind you," went on Ashley. "She seems to have got the whole thing under her belt this week. She's almost ready to hit the road."

"Really?"

"*I'm* not," he groaned. "I haven't even learnt the second act yet."

"Oh, dear," she said, wondering if she should smile or frown at his incompetence.

Mark turned from the coffee tray with a mug in his hands.

"Coffee, Ashley," he smiled.

Ashley looked up at him, coldly. "A cup in future please," he said, firmly. "I don't drink out of mugs."

Slowly, the rehearsal-room began to fill with members of the cast and chorus, all grabbing coffee and chattering excitedly. Having first greeted their two new fellow-understudies, several members of the chorus found a space to run through the minor parts which they had been employed to understudy as well.

Becky Masters, accompanied by the director, finally entered.

"Darling!" Ashley called. He crossed the room to greet her with a kiss.

Mark looked at Natasha for comfort. She shrugged and gave him a sympathetic smile before she allowed her eyes to follow the handsome Ashley Gibson.

The principals, having broken for lunch at one o'clock, hurried from the rehearsal room to the nearest pub. Natasha grabbed for her coat, intending to follow them.

The kindly stage manager called to her, "Not you, Natasha. You and Mark have to reset the props for scene three."

"Oh." Her cheeks reddened. "Sorry. I didn't realize."

He smiled at her. "It'll only take about fifteen minutes," he said, softly. "Then you can take a break. But back at two, eh?"

"Right," she replied.

The stage manager left the ASMs to their work.

Mark approached Natasha. "I didn't realize that being assistant stage managers meant that we were total dogsbodies," he moaned.

She grinned. "Me neither." She picked up a small vase containing fake flowers from the prop table. "Can you remember where these go?"

He laughed. "On the coffee table, centre stage," he informed her, adding, "I can see you're going to be terribly efficient at this job, Natasha."

She laughed too. "I'm just a bit confused," she said. "I'll be okay when we've done it a few times."

She crossed to the coffee table and placed the vase on it. Mark followed her and pushed it slightly to one side.

"There," he said. "A bit to the left. And the ashtray sits in front of it."

Natasha stared at him, wide-eyed. "How do you know?"

"Retentive memory," he smiled. "Like learning lines. I've only got to look at them, and I know them."

"Well, *I* can do that," she said. "Learning lines is no problem. But then, that's because it's what I *want* to do."

"Meaning, you don't want to ASM?" he asked her.

"Do *you*?" she asked him.

"Do I hell!" he replied. "But if it's going to get me work in the theatre, then so be it."

"Do you think we'll ever get to play the parts?" she mused.

"For real?"

"Yes."

"I doubt it," he replied. "They both look quite healthy, don't they?"

Natasha stopped herself from informing Mark that Becky Masters had a reputation for unreliability.

"No. We won't play them," he went on. "We'll be lucky if we even get to rehearse them."

Natasha began to panic. "But we *have* to rehearse," she said. "Suppose we're suddenly called to take over?"

Mark shrugged. "I expect the company manager will take us for a few rehearsals, but basically we'll have to do it ourselves. You and me. We'll have to watch what Ashley and Becky are doing, and then copy them."

"What do you think of her?" Natasha asked.

"Becky Masters?"

"Yes."

"She's beautiful."

"Yes, but what about her acting?"

"She's very good. Don't you think so?"

She hesitated. "Um? Yes. She's very good. I think."

"And what about Ashley?" Mark asked, with a twinkle in his eye.

"He's the most beautiful, sexiest, hunkiest guy I've ever seen," she replied, twinkling back.

"But he can't act," said Mark. "He's awful. I can't believe it. And he was so good in *Outback*."

"He'll probably improve with a bit more rehearsal," said Natasha. "Don't you think?"

Mark changed the subject. "Hey, let's get on with this set-up and then we can join them for lunch, eh?"

"Right," she said. "Where do I set the candlesticks, Mark?"

He grinned. "I'll do it. You tidy up the coffee corner."

They tried the nearest pub and found the company gathered around three small tables, tucking into bar meals. Ashley was deep in conversation with the director, Bill Grant, while the other principals were chatting over their salads and ploughman's lunches.

Becky Masters sat alone, looking at her script, while sipping on a vodka and tonic.

"I'll get them," said Natasha as soon as they entered the bar. "What would you like?"

"Half of bitter, please," replied Mark. He looked around the crowded bar, wondering where they were going to sit.

The stage manager sidled up to them. "All set?" he asked.

"Yes," replied Mark. "No problem. Except we weren't quite sure where to put the photo frame."

He thought for a while. "It goes on the sideboard, I think," he said, unsure.

"Oh, I know it goes on the sideboard," replied Mark, "but I couldn't remember which end."

The stage manager laughed. "It doesn't matter," he said. He patted Mark on the back. "I can see you're going to be great at this job." He turned to Natasha, who was just paying for the ordered drinks. "And how about you, Natasha?" he asked.

"She's an expert," interrupted Mark. "She's much better than me."

"Good one," smiled the stage manager. He looked at his watch. "I'll see you back there in half an hour then? I'm going to make some phone calls."

He left.

"Do you want anything to eat, Mark?" asked Natasha.

"No. I'll eat tonight," he replied. "After the rehearsal. Apparently there's a cheap pasta place round the corner."

"Really?" she said, enthusiastically. "Can I come with you?" She bit on her lip, feeling embarrassed. "Sorry. You're probably meeting someone there, are you?"

"No," he said. "I'd love you to come with me. That'd be great."

Natasha stared across at the group of gathered actors and caught Ashley Gibson's eye. He winked and smiled at her, before returning to his conversation with Bill Grant.

She shivered excitely.

Mark saw the look between them … and ignored it.

"Nowhere to sit," sighed Natasha, who wished she could join the rest of the cast.

"Unless we join Becky Masters," he suggested, jokingly.

"Why not?" said Natasha, as she began to approach Becky's table.

"I wouldn't," whispered Mark. "She's studying her script."

"She won't mind," said Natasha, confidently.

Becky Masters looked up.

"Can we join you?" asked Natasha.

Becky stared at her, quizzically. "Sorry, darling?"

"Do you mind if we sit here?"

"Isn't there anywhere else?" asked Becky.

Natasha suddenly felt very uncomfortable. "Well … I…"

"Sorry, darling," added Becky. "I just don't feel like talking. I'm trying to work."

Mark grabbed Natasha's arm. "It's okay, Natasha," he said. "We can stand at the bar."

He led Natasha away from the table, having given an unreturned smile to Becky Masters.

"How embarrassing," blushed Natasha. "She looked at me as though I was something the cat dragged in."

"Forget it," whispered Mark. "She's probably worried about her part."

"But there was no need to be quite so rude, was there?"

"No, there wasn't," agreed Mark. "But you must've heard about Becky Masters? Everyone knows she's highly strung."

Natasha grimaced. "She's going to be great fun on tour, isn't she? I hope I don't have to share digs with her."

Mark laughed. "Digs?"

"What's so funny?"

"You'll be in digs, Natasha. And so will I. But Becky Masters won't. She'll be in a hotel. Along with Ashley Gibson." He looked at his watch. "Let's get back, eh?" he suggested. "We can make some coffee before the stars come out to play."

3

"Well done, all!" yelled Bill Grant. "Let's call it a day, shall we?" He clapped his hands, enthusiastically. "I must say it's in jolly good shape."

"I hope you're not saying we're ready?" laughed Ashley Gibson. "I still haven't learnt the end of act two."

"Better learn it tonight, darling," Becky Masters called out, good-humouredly. "We're having a complete run-through tomorrow."

Ashley looked at Bill. "Is that right?"

"Apart from the musical numbers. Yes. So you'd better get to bed early tonight and take that script with you." He smiled. "Word perfect tomorrow please."

"You're a hard task-master," groaned Ashley, as he groped beneath the prop table for his bag.

Natasha nervously approached the director.

"Bill?"

"Yes, darling?"

"Have you any plans to rehearse the understudies this week?" she asked.

He put his arm around her and began propelling her towards the door. "I thought we'd let you settle in first," he explained. "Sort out all your ASM duties. Then we'll talk about rehearsing sometime next week. Okay?"

"Yes. Thanks," she said, realizing that this meant there'd be just a week's rehearsal for the understudies before the show went out on tour. "Thanks, Bill."

He smiled at her and called after Becky Masters. "Becky? Drinkies before you set off home?"

"That'd be lovely, darling," she said.

They left arm in arm.

Natasha quietly returned to the prop table, where Mark was setting out props, in order, for act one.

"I thought if we did this now, it'd save us time in the morning before the run-through," he explained.

"Did you hear what he said?" asked Natasha.

"Bill?"

"Yes."

"Yes. We're not rehearsing till next week."

"Doesn't give us much time, does it? We haven't even *heard* three of the songs yet."

"Don't worry," replied Mark. "You and I will have to get in early in the mornings. And stay till late at night if needs be. We can rehearse it on our own. The moves aren't that complicated."

"And when are the other understudies joining?" asked Natasha. "We'll have to work it all out with them."

Mark looked at her, amazed. "Are you serious?" he asked.

"What do you mean?"

"There aren't any other understudies, Natasha," he informed her. "All the smaller parts are covered by the chorus. It's only you and me who've got the replacement show on our shoulders."

"No other understudies?" she gasped.

"That's right," said a voice behind her.

She turned to see Ashley Gibson grinning at her.

"Did I leave my script on the prop table?" he asked. Mark picked up the dog-eared script and handed it to him.

"The management wouldn't be able to afford to employ more than two understudies." He winked at her, totally ignoring Mark. "But don't you worry your pretty little head. You'll be just fine."

He placed his script into his bag and left, calling, "See you tomorrow."

Natasha looked at Mark and shrugged.

"How does he know what the management can afford?" wondered Mark.

"He *is* the management, that's why," said Natasha.

Mark laughed. "He never is!"

"He's got money invested in the show," explained Natasha. "He told me. He must be part of Coy Productions."

"You *believe* that?"

"Why shouldn't I?"

"Because I'm *telling* you," said Mark, seriously. "I know who owns this show, lock, stock and barrel … and Ashley Gibson is simply a hired actor. Nothing more. Take it from me."

"You must tell me more," giggled a curious Natasha. "Over our spaghetti bolognese."

Ashley Gibson returned to the rehearsal room.

"I'd forget my head if it wasn't screwed on," he said. He crossed to one of the tubular chairs and picked up his umbrella. "It's pouring down out there," he said. "God, I love your English weather."

As he crossed the room, he turned to call to Natasha. "Had anything to eat today?"

"Er … no…" she replied.

"I'm going for a meal and a couple of glasses of wine. Do you want to join me?"

Natasha looked at Mark … who immediately looked away.

"Er … yes. Thanks. That'd be great," she replied. "I've just got to finish setting up these props."

"Your partner in crime can do that, can't he?"

"Yes, go on," said Mark. "I'll do it. I'll see you in the morning."

"Are you sure?" she half whispered.

"Of course he's sure," said Ashley. "Come on, darling. I'm famished."

Natasha grabbed for her coat and her bag and hurried for the door, giving a glance back to Mark, who was already busy resetting the props.

Le Piat in Soho was empty; its waiters still preparing for the onslaught of the pre-theatre goers.

"We'll have the quiet corner table as usual,

26

please, Pierre," Ashley told the waiter.

The waiter led them to a small table in an alcove, cosy and redly lit.

Natasha smiled, knowingly. "As usual?" she enquired.

"Business meetings," he assured her. "I don't usually bring my dates here. I have to be tucked away into an alcove to stop the autograph hunters from disturbing me."

She said it without thinking. "Do they still bother you?"

His smile dropped, momentarily. "Yes, they still bother me," he replied. "I'm not quite a has-been yet, you know!"

"Oh, I didn't mean…"

"I only left the show a year ago," he went on. "And I still have many fans who wish I'd never left."

"Me for one," said Natasha, quickly, hoping that she hadn't hurt him. "I don't bother watching it now that you've left."

His grin widened, flashing a row of perfectly straight, gleaming white teeth. "That's nice to hear."

"It's true," she said. "Have you never thought of going back?"

"No," he replied, as he handed her a menu. "Never."

The waiter approached.

"We'll have a bottle of the house wine," he said. He looked across his menu at Natasha. "Is that all right with you? It's very good here. It's not some cheap plonk."

"Fine," she replied. "I don't drink much anyway. It gives me a headache."

He smiled at her. "And that's the last thing we want you to have tonight, isn't it?"

She looked up at him and returned the smile.

He was struck by her beauty, as he had been that first moment she'd entered for her audition.

Natasha could feel her heart pounding. She would never have dreamed it were possible. If anyone had told her, this time last year, that one day soon, she'd be sitting opposite her hero; the heart-throb star of *Outback* ... she would have dismissed the idea as pure fantasy. But here she was! And he was still smiling at her, those dark brown eyes almost devouring her.

"God, you're beautiful," he said.

She gulped and tried to brush off the remark with a coy turn of her blonde head.

"Really," he went on. "You must have had the guys at drama school falling over themselves to take you out."

She giggled. "I was too busy. More interested in my career."

"All work and no play," he said, "can make Jill a very dull girl, if she's not careful."

"I'm *very* careful!" she grinned provocatively.

The waiter arrived with the wine and poured a little into each of the glasses.

"Are you ready to order?" he asked.

"No. Not yet," Ashley replied.

The waiter left.

"And talking of work," said Natasha, "shouldn't you be at home learning your lines for act two?"

"Lines can wait," he replied. "How can I even think about work when I'm sitting opposite someone as beautiful as you?"

She decided to grab the opportunity to find out more about his monetary investment in the show.

"Still, I suppose if it's your show, you can do as you please," she said. "After all ... you're the boss."

"Not quite," he mumbled.

She looked at him, surprised.

"I know! I know!" he blurted out, guiltily. "I know what I said to you on the phone ... but it's not quite true."

"So you haven't invested any of your cash in this?"

"I'm on a percentage of the box-office takings," he tried to explain. "So, of course, if the show's a success, I make a packet. If it bombs ... I don't get a bean."

"I see," she said.

"So ... as I've invested so much of my time into it ... it *has* to work. I turned down an Australian mini-series to do this. A lot of dollars."

"I still don't see why *I* was so important to the production," she said. "There must be hundreds of actresses who can do what I'm doing."

He laughed. "Are you fishing for compliments?"

She felt very embarrassed. "No. Of course I'm not."

"Look, Natasha," he said, seriously, "we saw dozens of girls ... but none of them had anywhere near what you had to offer. Had this been some tacky little theatre tour, we'd have grabbed the cheapest ASM going; one that could sing well enough just to keep the curtain up if Becky Masters went sick. But we've bigger expectations than that for this production. We hope, after its tour, to take it into London. Then who knows? New York? It's possible. It's a great little show."

"Oh, I agree..."

"And there's no denying that Becky Masters will pull in the punters. She's very popular."

"Very."

"But we do have our concerns about her."

"I know," said Natasha. "I've heard quite a lot about her on the grapevine. It's not just what you told me on the phone."

"Well, then you understand," he continued. "She's a very difficult lady."

The waiter returned once again to their table, note-pad in hand.

"Still not ready," Ashley informed him. "Give us a few more minutes."

"Yes, sir," he replied, retreating once again.

"I think we'd better stop the chat for a minute and scour these menus," he told Natasha, "or else we'll be here all night." He grinned. "And that would never do."

They walked out into the busy streets of Soho and waited for a passing cab.

"It's stopped raining," sighed Natasha. "At last."

Ashley tutted. "Not exactly Bondi Beach weather though, is it?" He shivered. "I should've taken that mini-series," he joked. "At least I'd've kept warm."

A vacant taxi turned the corner and Ashley waved it down.

"Whereabouts do you live?" he asked Natasha as they waited for the taxi to pull up.

"Greenwich," she replied. "Do you know it?"

"I know *of* it," he said. "Greenwich Mean Time … and all that."

They climbed into the taxi.

"Where do *you* live?" she asked him. "I bet it's not south of the Thames?"

"No way, José," he laughed. "It has to be Central London for me."

"Have you got a flat?"

"An apartment? No. I'm in a hotel in Bayswater."

"Where to?" the cabbie asked.

"Bayswater," Ashley replied.

Natasha began to panic. It suddenly occurred to her that Ashley might be expecting her to join him in his hotel. It might only be for a nightcap, but even so … she had to get home. She wondered how she could tell him, without causing offence.

"Wouldn't it be best if the taxi went to Charing Cross first?" she asked. She checked her watch. "There's a train to Greenwich at quarter past."

He looked a bit surprised. "You want to go straight home?"

"I must," she replied. "Sorry. I hope you weren't expecting…?

Ashley called to the taxi driver. "Forget Bayswater," he said. "Make it Greenwich."

The cab spun round and made its way down towards the Embankment.

"Oh, but there's no need, Ashley," Natasha

31

protested. "It's ever such a long way. It'll cost a fortune by cab."

"Nonsense," he replied.

"I can just as easily catch the train."

"Quiet," he said, softly. He put his arm around her shoulders and pulled her closer. "The longer the journey, the more time I get to be alone with you." He nodded towards the driver. "Well ... *almost* alone," he laughed.

The taxi pulled up, as instructed, in Montello Road. Ashley helped Natasha from the back seat and then, to her surprise, he paid the driver.

"That was a bit daft, wasn't it?" said Natasha as the taxi headed back for London.

Ashley wrapped his arms around her and kissed her, passionately. Natasha felt her heart racing once again as her most secret childhood fantasies about the delicious Ashley Gibson came flooding back. She could hardly believe that this was happening to her. His kiss was just as she'd always imagined it; tender and warm. So, so warm.

He pulled back and looked at her, almost smothering her with the loving stare from his dreamy dark eyes.

"How do you mean?" he asked. "A bit daft?"

"You've let the taxi go," she replied. "And they're not easy to find in the streets of Greenwich."

"Oh, dear," he smirked. "What a shame. That means I'll have to stay here, won't I?"

She stared at him, wide-eyed; shocked at the presumption. "You can't," she said.

"Come on," he purred. "You know you want me to. Stop playing games."

"I'm sorry," she said, gently but firmly. "You can't."

He suddenly realized. "Don't tell me you live with your parents?" He sighed deeply.

"Yes," she replied. "As a matter of fact, I do. But I don't see that that's got anything to do with it, Ashley. Even if I lived on my own, the answer would still be no."

He looked at her aghast. "What?"

She turned away from him and began to walk up the path to her front door.

"Good night, Ashley!" she called back.

"Good night," he replied, in a hushed voice, sounding surprised and hurt.

As she reached her door, she turned and saw him standing like a forlorn little boy under the street lamp.

"Thanks for a lovely evening," she called, sincerely. "It was really, really nice."

He gave her the flicker of a smile.

"You're welcome," he replied softly. "We must do it again sometime."

4

"So, how was it for you?" Mark asked facetiously as Natasha hurried breathlessly through the door.

"The train was late," gasped Natasha. "Has anyone missed me?"

Mark looked at his watch. "You're not late."

"Aren't I?" She was surprised.

"We weren't called till half-past."

She sighed, relieved. "Thank goodness for that." She crossed to the coffee corner. "Want one?"

"Please." He asked again ... more delicately this time. "How did you get on with lover-boy?"

"We had a nice meal," she replied. "And then he took me home in a cab. All the way to Greenwich." She looked up and grinned at Mark's expressionless face.

"I bet he did," he said.

"Actually," she confessed, "it was all a bit difficult. I think he had every intention of meeting the in-laws." She laughed.

"But he didn't?"

"He didn't. I sent him packing. I don't think he was very pleased."

Mark joined her at the steaming kettle and idly flicked a sweetener into his mug.

"So you didn't like him then?" he asked, sounding only half-interested.

"I liked him, yes," she replied. "Actually, I still think he's divine, but…"

"It was just a meal."

"Precisely."

As the cast began to amble into the rehearsal room thirty minutes later, Natasha continually kept her eye on the door for Ashley. He was the last to arrive and he immediately crossed the room to talk to Bill Grant.

"I'll have to use my script for the end of the play, Bill," he said. "Sorry. I was up until three trying to cram home these lines, but they haven't quite sunk in yet."

Bill Grant gave a stern headmaster's look to the actor.

"Really sorry," added Ashley. "I'll know them by tomorrow morning. I promise."

Bill clapped his hands to call to attention all the actors assembled. "Okay, boys and girls," he said. "Let's get set up for act one."

Ashley took off his mac as he crossed to the coffee corner. Natasha stood at the prop table, checking off the prop-list with Mark. She waited for Ashley to look across at her. He turned, caught her eye and looked away again.

"I think you may have hurt Mr Outback's ego, don't you?" whispered Mark.

"Mark!" called Ashley. "A coffee when you've finished over there. In a cup, please!"

As the cast broke for lunch, Natasha and Mark reset the props and furniture once again for act one. Bill Grant was delighted that the musical director, who'd been splitting his time between this show and an earlier contracted fringe-cabaret, was now free to give all his attention to *A Stranger Love*. He'd be arriving at two o'clock to take the company slowly through the ten numbers of the show.

"Do you know your lines?" Mark asked, as he helped Natasha move the chaise-longue to its act-one centre-stage position.

"Of course. Don't you?" puffed Natasha. "This is really heavy," she added. "Can I put it down?"

They placed down the weighty piece of furniture and Mark dragged it further upstage to its rightful position.

"Yes," he said. "I know all my lines too. So ... I was thinking, Natasha ... why don't we come in early tomorrow and rehearse our scenes together?"

"Why not?" she replied. She returned to the prop table to pick up a large ashtray. "Where does this go?" she asked.

He tutted and took it from her with a smile. "I'll do it."

She sighed. "He didn't look at me once. Totally ignored me."

Mark shrugged. "He's just buried in his work.

He's got a lot to learn and if you ask me, he's terrified."

Natasha was surprised at the comment. "Do you think so?"

"I'm sure so. That's why he puts on that great act. He's trembling inside, believe me."

He wiped the ashtray with a duster and placed it on the low, marble-topped table.

"Then why does he spend most of his time ordering the rest of the cast around?" asked Natasha.

Mark grinned. "I notice he doesn't order Becky Masters around."

"She'd floor him," laughed Natasha.

"She's very good, isn't she?" said Mark.

"A good actress," agreed Natasha. "But I wonder if she can sing."

Mark raised a questioning eyebrow. "We'll find out this afternoon, won't we?"

Becky Masters *could* sing. Most of the cast were shocked at just how *well* she could sing.

Ashley Gibson's mouth dropped open as Becky plunged into the opening lines of the show's title number, *A Stranger Love*.

Aching hearts are breaking; caring
  For nothing around me, while I'm sharing
A stranger's love.

For the first time that day, he acknowledged Natasha, who was leaning against the prop table, listening in awe to the incredible voice resounding off the rehearsal room's dusty rafters. He smiled at her and winked. Natasha smiled back.

"Well, that was really cool, wasn't it?" said Mark, the following morning.

Natasha had arrived five minutes before him and had filled and switched on the kettle.

"What are you talking about?"

"I suppose he took you all the way home again?"

Natasha giggled. "We went for a drink, that's all. I only stayed half an hour ... then I went to catch my train."

"You should've turned him down," said Mark.

"Why? I like him."

Mark mumbled, "Gets everything he wants. He's just got to snap his fingers and everyone comes running."

Natasha stared at Mark. She thought, at first, that he was joking, but she could now see from his expression that he was irritated.

"Actually, we weren't alone when we went for our drink," she informed him. "Becky Masters came into the bar and joined us."

"Oh?"

"And guess who she was talking about?"

Mark began to put coffee into their mugs. "I've no idea."

"You!" she said.

He looked up at her. "Me?"

"Yes. She was very strange. She wanted to know all about you. She was asking me lots of questions."

He replied nonchalantly, "Perhaps she fancies me."

Natasha eyed Mark, suspiciously. Surely he wasn't serious? He was a very nice person ... or appeared to be, from the very short time she'd known him ... but he was hardly suitable material for someone as beautiful as Becky Masters.

"Although with someone like Ashley Gibson around, she's not likely to go for someone like me, is she?" he added quickly.

"Well..."

"So how much did you tell her?" he asked.

She was about to reply, "not much," when he answered his own question.

"Couldn't really tell her anything, could you? Because you don't know anything about me, do you?" He looked up at her and smiled ... a very warm, comforting smile. "But you could find out. Possibly." He laughed. "Depends how hard you try."

"Well! Well! Well! We are keen this morning," said a voice from the door.

Mark and Natasha turned to face a grinning Ashley Gibson.

"I thought I'd come in early to go through my lines," he explained. "Didn't think you two would be here already."

"Mark and I are going to run through our scenes together," said Natasha. "This is the only opportunity we get."

"Well, you don't want me watching you, do you?" Ashley asked rhetorically.

"No," said Mark, quickly.

"So I'll go to the café for breakfast," added Ashley. "Good luck, folks."

Natasha waited until he'd left. "Perhaps we should have let him watch us," she said. "It might have shocked him to see that his understudy was better than him."

Mark shivered. "Don't say that," he pleaded. "You haven't seen me do it yet. I might be terrible."

Natasha smiled, gently took his hand and led him towards the chaise-longue. They sat and stared into each other's eyes, ready for the curtain to rise on act one.

She had the first line.

"So how long will you be away?"

He replied, glowering at her, "Look, Sarah, don't let's start all this again."

She stood and walked downstage. "I'm not starting anything, Jonathan. It's a simple question."

"And I don't know the answer!" He remained seated.

"You mean you've no intention of telling me!" She turned on him. "Why can't you be honest? Why don't you just say that you're meeting her in Paris?"

He stood, stunned. "What?"

"I *know*, Jonathan!" she said. She began to cry. "I know all about it, so let's stop the pretence."

There was a pause.

"Your line," said Natasha.

"Is it?" Mark was surprised. "I thought you were supposed to cross to the fireplace and say, 'You're treating me like a fool, Jonathan.'"

"Oh!" said Natasha. "Sorry. You're right. Can we go back a bit?"

They returned to Sarah's sudden turn on Jonathan.

SARAH: Why can't you be honest? Why don't you just say that you're meeting her in Paris?

JONATHAN STANDS, STUNNED.

JONATHAN: What?

SARAH: I *know*, Jonathan! (CRIES) I know all about it, so let's stop the pretence.

SHE CROSSES TO THE FIREPLACE

You're treating me like a fool, Jonathan.

"Not bad at all," called Ashley Gibson from the back of the room. Mark jumped. Natasha giggled.

"Café's closed," shrugged Ashley. "Don't mind me. You carry on."

"I think we'll leave it," grumbled Mark. "We'll have another go tomorrow, Natasha." He crossed towards the coffee corner. "Coffee, Ashley?" he asked.

Ashley laughed. "Oh, come on!" he said. "You two carry on. I'm not inhibiting you. I'll just sit here and read my script."

Natasha was keen to continue. "Come on, Mark."

"I'd rather not," Mark replied softly.

"If you're going to be put off with just one other person in the room," suggested Ashley, "what are you going to be like with a theatre full of eager punters?"

"It's not the same thing!" snapped Mark. "I shall be *ready* by then. If I ever have to play it, that is."

"Not if you don't rehearse, you won't," grinned Ashley.

"Please, Mark!" pleaded Natasha.

But Mark was adamant. "No!"

"I'll do it with you," said Ashley to Natasha.

Natasha was unsure, especially having seen Mark's startled reaction.

"Well, I..."

"Let's go from the beginning of act two," hurried on Ashley. "It'll help me as well, 'cause that's where I'm a bit sticky on my lines."

"I'm going to buy a newspaper," said Mark, his voice trembling.

"No! I want you here!" called Ashley. "You can follow the book to see where I go wrong." He flung his script across the room to Mark. "Here."

"I'm going for a walk!" said Mark.

"No, you're not!" said Ashley, firmly. "You're the ASM, son ... and this is part of your job. I want you to follow the book. So come and sit down here – " he pointed to the director's chair – "and turn to act two."

Mark stalked across the room and slumped into the chair, flicking angrily through the script until he came to the correct page.

Natasha's face had flushed bright red. Her loyalties to both work-mates were divided. She wanted to run through with her possible future leading man, and this was an ideal opportunity … but she felt sorry for Mark, who was being treated appallingly.

"As the scene opens, we're in each other's arms," lectured Ashley. "By the fireplace."

"By the coffee table, actually!" snapped Mark.

Ashley crossed to the coffee table without replying. Natasha joined him.

"So, let's start," said Ashley. He took Natasha in his arms.

JONATHAN: If it were the other way round, I'm not sure that I could forgive you.

SARAH: It hasn't been easy.

JONATHAN: I know. I'm sorry, Sarah. I know you'll find this difficult to believe, but I've never stopped loving you. Never.

SARAH: Oh, Jonathan.

HE KISSES HER.

The kiss made Natasha's legs feel weak. She kept telling herself, you're *acting*, Natasha. And so is he.

And still the kiss went on.

Mark looked up from the script. "Too long!" he said. Ashley stopped the kiss and glared across at Mark.

"What did you say?" he fumed.

"The kiss was too long. You don't spend that long doing it with Becky."

"I don't want you directing me, thank you!" yelled Ashley. "I just want you to follow the book and make sure I get the lines right!"

Mark stood and threw the script to the floor.

"Follow your own bloody book!" he said as he stormed out of the room.

5

Mark returned to the rehearsal room just before the run-through was about to start, and throughout the morning he received sympathetic looks from Natasha and furious glares from Ashley Gibson.

During the short coffee break, Natasha quickly finished her prop setting and hurried to Mark's side to offer him solace. Before she had a chance to speak, one of the chorus approached; a large woman with a dark brown voice who was understudying the tiny part of Mrs Kempton, the housekeeper.

"I've just been struck by a terrible pang of guilt," she expostulated. "I forgot to give you an invitation, didn't I?"

"An invitation?" queried Natasha.

"I never usually forget the ASMs," she continued. "Never. I don't know what came over me."

Mark and Natasha looked at each other. What was she talking about?

"My celebratory bash," she explained. "A little cast party at my house this evening. A sort of birthday-do and a good luck send-off for the show."

"Oh … happy birthday," said Natasha, who wasn't quite sure how to react.

"Well, my birthday isn't for a couple of weeks yet," explained the actress, "but we'll be in Brighton by then. In some beastly digs I expect. So I decided to throw the party tonight. All the cast are coming and it would be just too, too awful if you two didn't join us."

Natasha was taken aback. "Well, I'm not sure …"

"Oh please don't say you can't make it," whined the actress. "I feel so, so guilty about not inviting you sooner."

"Is it far?" asked Natasha.

"Fulham, darling," she replied. "Not far at all."

Natasha laughed. "It's quite far from Greenwich. I'd have to call my parents and tell them I'll be late back."

"But you will come?"

Natasha looked at Mark. "Can *you* make it?"

He shrugged. "Don't see why not. But I'll have to ring my girlfriend in Peckham to tell her I'll be late."

Natasha was taken by surprise. She knew that Mark had a flat in Peckham, but it had never crossed her mind that he might be living with a girlfriend.

"Oh, I *am* pleased," shrieked the actress. "I'll give you the address later. The bash starts about eight-thirty."

She flashed them a beaming smile before crossing the room to join her fellow-actors for coffee.

"You're a dark horse," said Natasha to Mark. "You didn't say you had a girlfriend."

"You didn't ask," grinned Mark, adding quickly, "You've put those candlesticks in the wrong place again."

Mark stood with his back to the sink, refusing to leave the kitchen and join the party.

"But we've got to socialize," said Natasha. "How do you expect to get decent parts in the theatre if you can't even chat to the director you're working with?"

"You go and chat to him," mumbled Mark. "He's talking to Ashley Gibson and I don't want to be anywhere near him."

Natasha did. She couldn't wait to get near Ashley Gibson.

"So what did you think of the run-through?" Ashley asked Bill Grant.

Bill sipped at his wine and said nothing.

"You weren't being honest, were you?" Ashley pushed him into a reply.

"I said it was good," shrugged Bill. "And I meant it." He looked long and hard at Ashley. "But it's not West End material. Not yet, anyway."

Ashley gasped. "You're joking? I'm only doing it so's I can do a run in London."

"I know. And I need the West End credit too," sighed Bill. "But quite honestly, it's not another

Andrew Lloyd Webber. We'll be lucky if we sell out in the provinces. Advance bookings in Brighton could've been much better."

Ashley shook his head in dismay.

"Look," said Bill. "I might be wrong, Ashley. I went to the first night of *Cats* and I said it wouldn't run. So who am I to judge?"

"When are the management coming?" asked Ashley, knowing that Coy Productions would have the final say on a West End transfer.

"Not till we run the show in Brighton," explained Bill. "Sam Coy's got a West End theatre already lined up ... but you know Sam. He'll never pour money into something that's not an absolute certainty."

"We've got to make it work," said Ashley determinedly. He looked at the clock on the living-room wall. "I'd better get off," he said. "I'm expecting a call from Sydney at eleven."

Bill tried to lighten the atmosphere. "Give him my love," he said.

"Who?"

"Sydney."

Ashley grinned. "Oh, by the way," he said. "That ASM lad ... the one who's understudying me..."

"Mark Fallon?"

"Yes."

"What about him?"

"What's he like? As an actor, I mean?"

"Very good. Or he was at the audition. Why?"

"No chance in replacing him then?"

Bill was stunned. "Whatever for?"

Ashley sighed deeply. "Don't know. There's

48

something about him I don't like."

Bill smiled. "You mean he hasn't jumped to your demands, eh?"

"Arrogant little…"

Bill noted that the actor's eyes were flaring.

"Now, now," said Bill. He placed his hand on Ashley's arm. "He can't be that bad."

"Couldn't you have a word with him? Tell him to watch his step. Or I might just put one on him."

"I *wouldn't*," warned Bill. He lowered his voice, whispering. "Can't say too much at this stage, Ashley … but let's just say that young Mark Fallon came to us highly recommended by Coy Productions."

Natasha peered through into the living-room and saw that Ashley was bidding good night to the hostess.

"Oh … he's leaving," groaned Natasha. She looked at her watch. "And it's only ten-thirty."

"He's probably as bored as I am," grinned Mark. "But being the star, he can leave when he wants to. We've got to be a bit more polite."

Natasha tutted. "What's the matter with you? It's not boring. The food's wonderful."

"It's hardly a rave, is it?" argued Mark. "Background sixties' music doesn't really excite me."

Natasha reached for an opened bottle of white wine and poured some into Mark's glass.

"Thanks," he smiled at her. "I feel better already."

"So where do you and your girlfriend go for fun, then?" she asked him. "You don't really go to raves, do you?"

"What girlfriend?" asked Mark with a sly look.

"You haven't got a girlfriend, have you?"

"Haven't I?"

"*Have* you?"

"Why do you want to know?" He was playing with her; a cat and mouse game of which she didn't approve.

"I *don't*," she said. "I *don't* want to know." She huffily flicked back her blonde hair. "You're a strange one," she said, shaking her head. "You're so secretive."

"Am I?" He smiled, broadly.

"I was going to ask you if we could share digs on the tour, but I don't know anything about you. I don't know if I could live with you."

He stopped smiling. "You could find out a lot more about me, if you spent more time talking to me and less time looking at Mr Outback," he said, softly.

She looked straight into his eyes. She noted their wishy-washy colouring. Not quite green, not quite blue. Sort of greyish. Not like the beautiful dark brown eyes belonging to Ashley Gibson. And yet, somehow, there seemed to be more life behind these eyes. They were, curiously, despite their colouring, warmer ... friendlier than Ashley's.

"I'm going to have a word with Bill," she said quickly. "Coming?"

"No," he replied. "I'm staying here for a bit. *You* go."

"I'm freeing the cast at lunchtime tomorrow," Bill

informed her. "And then I'll work with the understudies. It's not before time."

"Thanks," replied Natasha. "It's just that I was getting a bit worried. If I have to go on ... I'm nowhere near prepared."

"I hear you worked this morning with Ashley," he said.

Natasha was surprised. "Who told you?"

"A little birdie," grinned Bill. "It's a good idea, darling. After all, if you have to go on, it'll be Ashley you'll be working with. Not Mark."

"Unless Ashley's off too."

"I doubt it," he said.

She asked, quietly ... confidentially, "Do you think Becky Masters is likely to be off?"

He winked at her. "Just learn those lines, Natasha, and rehearse them over and over again. That's all I'm prepared to say."

She nodded, excitedly. "Oh, I will."

"Now what's going on between Ashley and Mark?" he asked. "I hear they had a little confrontation.

"I'm not sure," she replied. "They certainly don't like each other, but I don't know why."

"You don't think it's because Mark's got the hots for you, do you?"

She laughed. "No. I'm sure he hasn't."

"Only I know Ashley has."

"Has he?"

"He took you out I hear ... on the first day of rehearsal."

"You don't miss much, do you?" she asked.

He laughed, heartily. "Not much, darling."

She became serious. "I think he's wonderful," she sighed. "I've always thought so."

"And Mark?"

"Pardon?"

"What do you think of Mark?"

She hadn't really thought about it. Not seriously. "Mark's just Mark," she shrugged. "He's nice. I think he'll make a good friend. Especially when we're on tour."

Natasha returned to the kitchen some thirty minutes later and was shocked to find Mark's arms wrapped around Becky Masters.

He looked over Becky's shoulder at the gawping Natasha.

"Hi!" he said. "Thought you'd disappeared for good."

Becky pulled away and turned to face Natasha. Her face was tear-streaked.

"Sorry," she said as she hurried from the kitchen, brushing past an amazed Natasha.

"What's the matter with her?" asked Natasha.

Mark sighed. "A few emotional problems. She's quite upset."

Natasha went to his side, whispering, "What about?"

"I can't tell you," replied Mark. "She told me in confidence."

"Well, you two seemed to be getting on great guns," she said, surprised. "Why on Earth would she want to tell *you* her problems?"

"Meaning?"

"You're hardly the best of mates are you? She's

totally ignored us so far."

"I know," he smiled, confidently. "But I think she's just a bit shy, that's all."

Natasha was speechless.

"I can't believe that you've done so well!" shouted Bill Grant to all the understudies, most of whom were members of *A Stranger Love*'s chorus. "That's almost a show you've given me! And you haven't had any proper rehearsal time! Excellent."

The understudy cast beamed.

"And what about Natasha?" enthused Bill.

Everyone applauded.

Natasha's cheeks reddened.

"Brilliant," said Bill. "And Mark – " he added quickly – "that's coming on really well."

The Musical Director, having arrived just as the rehearsal had finished, walked across to his piano. "But now we'll sort out the men from the boys," he said.

"Quite!" laughed Bill. "Excellent play! Wonderful acting, boys and girls. But this isn't a play, as you all know. It's a musical ... and now that we've got our illustrious MD with us ... let's rehearse the numbers."

A very ragged rendition of most of the songs made the MD cringe at his piano keys. And it wasn't until they came to the love duet, the title song from the musical, that he realized why he'd helped to cast these two young actors. Natasha sang the first two lines, beautifully:

Aching hearts are breaking; caring
  For nothing around me, while I'm sharing
A stranger's love.

Then Mark's voice, powerful and haunting, filled the rehearsal room:

And though you mean the world to me;
  To the world there could never be
A stranger love.

All heads turned and stared at the lad, hardly able to believe the incredible sound soaring from his mouth. Mark Fallon made Ashley Gibson sound like a cat on hot bricks. Natasha's mouth dropped open. Her body began to tremble violently. Excitedly. Singing with a leading man like this was everything an actress could dream of. His voice was simply ... the best she'd ever heard.

At the end of the number, the cast screamed their approval.

"Superb!" gushed the MD.

Bill Grant grabbed the lad's hand. "Fantastic," he said. "Absolutely fantastic."

"Thanks," said Mark.

Bill turned to the assembled actors.

"Well, what can I say?" he asked. "Let's call it a day, eh? We'll go through it all again on Friday afternoon ... after I've dismissed the main cast. Saturday you can have a free day ... to pack your bags etc ... and then we'll try to get another understudy run when we hit Brighton. If there's time. See you tomorrow, folks. And well done!"

Bill left the room, followed in dribs and drabs by the rest of the actors.

"Back to reality," Mark grinned at Natasha. "Let's sort out this prop table, shall we?"

She stared at him. "You were brilliant," she gasped. "I couldn't believe it."

"Thanks," he said, softly. "I can *sing* all right. I'm not worried about the numbers." He laughed. "It's the bits in between I can't do. All the acting bits!"

"Don't be silly," she said. "Of course you can. You only need some more rehearsals."

"A *lot* more rehearsals!"

"Look, why don't we stay on for another couple of hours?" she suggested. "We can go through some of the more difficult scenes. Work on them until they're right."

He looked embarrassed. "Well ... the truth is, Natasha," he said, "I've already arranged to go through the scenes ... with someone else."

"Oh?" she was taken aback. "Who?"

The door opened and Becky Masters flounced in.

6

For several minutes Natasha stared at Mark, who was sleeping soundly, oblivious to the beautiful countryside all around them. And as the train sped on through the Sussex Downs, nearing its destination, she wondered if she should wake him.

She'd had plenty of time during the past three days to ponder over Bill's statement about Mark being keen on her. Before Bill had made the comment, it hadn't occurred to her that Mark's dislike for Ashley might have been caused by jealousy. She was sure that Bill was wrong. Mark thought of her as nothing more than a friend. He couldn't possibly be jealous of Ashley. She was sure of that. But it *had* made Natasha curious. It had made her look at Mark with fresh eyes. And looking at him anew, she realized that she liked what she saw. And the feeling disturbed her.

"Mark," she whispered softly. "Mark."

He didn't wake. A muscle in his cheek flickered.

She watched him sleep on.

It was such a pity that he now spent all his free time rehearsing with Becky Masters. Natasha had hardly any time with him now.

And she missed him.

She'd liked his company.

And now she missed him.

"Mark?"

He opened his eyes, yawned, stretched and sat up in his seat.

"Sorry," he said. "I must've dozed off."

She laughed. "You've been sleeping like a baby for ages."

The train suddenly began to slow. Mark stood and dragged his over-packed bag from the rack. "We must be there," he said.

Natasha reached for her bag too. "And the sun has come out to greet us," she smiled.

"A Summer Sunday on the coast," he beamed. "What could be nicer?"

I know what could make it *perfect*, she thought. But she said nothing.

"This is it," said Mark.

He and Natasha stood at the large, black door belonging to a grand, Regency-built, terraced house. Mark rang the bell.

It was opened a short while later by a rotund man in his fifties. His face was jolly and puffy-red, matching his pillar-box coloured sweater.

"My actors?" he bellowed, dramatically.

"Yes," smiled Natasha.

"Best theatre digs in Brighton," he wheezed as

he led them into the hall and up the wide staircase to the first landing.

"I'm glad to hear it," laughed Mark.

"That's because I'm a thespian myself, dear boy," added the landlord. "Well, I *was*. Gave it up to do a sensible job." He laughed loudly. "Landlord to the stars. That's what I am now."

"We're hardly stars," grinned Natasha.

"You will be," he replied quickly. *Too* quickly thought Natasha, who realized this was probably his standard line to all newly-arrived guests.

"In here," said the landlord, opening the door to the first room. "It's got a nice dressing-table and hairdrier and dried flowers and things. So that's obviously – " he winked at Natasha – "for *you*!"

How sexist, thought Natasha. She stared into the room. But how cosy, she guiltily added to her thoughts.

"That looks great," she said. "Thanks."

He then led them both to the room next door.

"And this is the man's room," he said as he flung open the door.

It looked almost the same as Natasha's room. Mark noted the dressing-table and the hairdrier and an equal amount of dried flowers.

The landlord grinned at Mark. "Flowers for you too," he puffed. "I hate any kind of sexism, don't you?"

"Er ... yes," stammered Mark.

The landlord flung his arms wide in an extravagant gesture suggesting he was capable of embracing the whole world between them.

"We're all the same!" he yelled to the heavens.

58

"Do you hear that, God? All equal! Even we eccentric old theatricals!"

Mark gave a quick glance at Natasha, who was biting her lip, trying hard not to laugh.

The landlord quickly turned to catch her. "You're allowed to laugh," he said kindly. "They all do. I don't mind."

One of Natasha's face-muscles visibly twitched.

"And down the corridor…" yelled the landlord, returning to his bellowed delivery and over-acted arm gestures, "… is the shared kitchen … bathroom … and loo!"

He headed for the staircase and made his descent, calling without looking back, "So unpack. Make yourselves at home. And then join me and Earl Grey in the lounge."

Natasha mouthed to Mark, "Earl Grey?"

Mark whispered back, "Tea … which tastes like perfume."

They both grimaced and scurried into their respective rooms.

"He's quite sweet, isn't he?" said Natasha.

"He's a nutcase," laughed Mark.

They both lay back on the pebbled beach, enjoying the weak rays of the sun.

Mark closed his eyes and half-dozed.

"Mark?" she asked.

"Mmm?"

"What time do we have to be at the theatre?"

"About seven," he mumbled dreamily.

She sat up, turned over and leaned on one elbow, looking at his face.

It had taken her by surprise. Never in her wildest dreams had she thought that she would begin to feel this way over the plain-looking, very ordinary boy she'd encountered on that first day. Now, he didn't seem so plain. Side by side with handsome Ashley Gibson, Mark couldn't come anywhere near the almost perfect Australian heart-throb for looks. But...!

She examined more closely the tiny, button nose and the smooth, soft lips which always seemed to be on the verge of smiling. She *loved* his smile. She loved the way his eyes lit up when he grinned at her and the way in which the tiny lines appeared at the side of those eyes ... like bright rays shooting out from the sun. She adored the tiny dimple in his chin and longed to gently place a fingertip there.

"Do you think we'll have to unload the props all by ourselves?" she asked.

"I've no idea," he replied softly.

"The lorry is arriving at six."

"Mmm."

"So if we're not needed till seven ... perhaps the theatre's own stage-management are unloading."

"Maybe." He sat up, suddenly. "What's the time?"

She looked her watch, squinting against the sun, beginning to shine more forcefully now.

"Two o'clock, nearly. Why? Do you want to go for something to eat?"

"No," he said. He leapt to his feet. "I'd said I'd meet Becky at her hotel at two."

She couldn't hide her disappointment. "You're not going to rehearse this afternoon?"

"No. I just said I'd meet her there for lunch, that's all."

"Oh!"

"So I'll see you later at the theatre," he said. He began to run up the beach towards the promenade.

"If you're late," she called after him, "I'm not doing it by myself!"

"I'll see you at seven!" he called back. "Be good!"

Having strolled down to the water's edge and back again, several times, Natasha climbed up to the promenade and slumped on to one of the wooden benches facing the sea. She looked out to the horizon and began to daydream. If only she'd not been so hasty during those early rehearsal-days. If only she'd taken more time to separate the not-so-obvious wheat from the well-disguised chaff.

The sports car pulled up in the road behind her and the driver leapt out, calling, "G'day!"

She turned.

"Ashley. Hi!"

He walked towards the bench and sat beside her.

"All alone?"

"Yes."

"No Mark?"

"He's gone to the hotel to meet Becky."

He grinned. "Aah, yes. Becky. Whatever does she see in him, I wonder?"

Natasha reacted defensively. "They're only rehearsing."

"Yeah. Sure."

They both watched as two children ran screaming excitedly along the beach, chasing a sea-wet, black mongrel.

"So. How's it going?" he asked her, finally. "All set for the technical run?"

"Not yet," she replied. "We haven't even unloaded the lorry yet. We're not due into the theatre until seven."

"I can't say I'm looking forward to tomorrow," he sighed. "I hate Techs."

"Tuesday'll be worse," she said. "A dress rehearsal and then…"

"The big one!" He gulped. "Opening night. I'll never be ready."

"Of course you will." She smiled at him, comfortingly. "You'll be very good."

"Thanks," he said, softly.

He looked at his watch. "Hey, you've got ages before you have to be at the theatre." He grabbed her hand. "Why don't we go for a drink or something? What about lunch?"

She felt she'd much rather be having lunch with Mark. But as Mark was lunching with Becky…

"Okay," she replied.

"Race you to the car!" he laughed.

Becky sat at a bar table and looked around. "Not a bad hotel, is it?" she said.

"Better than digs," replied Mark. "Not that mine are bad … but at least you've got more freedom here. I've got this feeling our landlord will be watching every move we make."

"I used to hate staying in digs," she confided. She raised her vodka and tonic. "Cheers, darling."

He lifted his beer – "Cheers" – and drank. "Not that you stayed in digs for much of your career," he went on. "You've been a star for years."

She laughed. "Not *that* many years, thank you."

"Oh, I didn't mean…"

"I'm not *that* much older than you, you know."

"No."

She leaned across the table and took his hand. "Mark," she said, sounding serious.

He knew immediately. "What? There's something wrong, isn't there?"

"Yes. There's a problem."

His reply was hardly audible. "Tell me."

7

There was no doubt in Natasha's mind that there was something very wrong with Mark. She hadn't seen him like that before and could only guess that there'd been some terrible row between him and Becky. She wanted to run after him, to comfort him, but Ashley was hurrying her through to the hotel's restaurant and chattering on and on about *A Stranger Love* and its possible future success. He, it appeared, hadn't even noticed Mark, brushing past them in the lobby.

The menu was basic fare, which displeased Ashley as he was less a steak and chips man ... more a connoisseur in Cordon Bleu cookery. Natasha ate little, toying with her salad, her mind elsewhere. She wondered at the amount of red wine Ashley consumed with his steak. Her glass remained untouched, yet by the end of the meal, he'd ordered and emptied two full bottles and was now sipping brandy with his coffee.

"I'm really worried though, you know, Natasha," he slightly slurred. "I don't think I'm up to playing this part of Jonathan. I don't really understand the character. He seems a bit strange to me."

"Well ... he's rather a complex character," she agreed, "but if you remember ... in about chapter four of the novel ... the author goes into his background. *That* really shows what he's all about."

"I haven't read the novel," confessed Ashley.

Natasha was shocked. "You haven't?"

"I hate reading books," he said. "They're so long-winded." He grinned at her across the table. "You're beautiful, you know."

She embarrassedly sipped her coffee.

He prodded for a response. "You are, you know."

"Thanks."

"I think we should go up to my room, don't you?" he suddenly blurted, beginning to sound quite drunk.

She looked at his sleepy eyes. Sleepy through too much alcohol.

"Don't be silly," she said, flatly.

He reached out and grabbed her hand. "I'm not being silly. You fancy me and I fancy you ... so what's wrong with that?"

She withdrew her hand. "Ashley, I think *you* should go to your room and lie down for a while. I'm going to the theatre."

She stood.

"Don't go," he pleaded, child-like. "I'm frightened."

She looked down at him. "Frightened?"

"About Tuesday. I'm frightened about Tuesday. I can talk to you about it. You make things sound better." He was really slurring his words now. "Don't go. Come upstairs with me."

"No, Ashley," she said firmly, but kindly. "There's nothing to be frightened about. You'll be marvellous."

"Don't then!" he said. He stood and swayed slightly before heading for the staircase. "Don't! See if I care!"

"Ashley," she called gently.

He turned, looking at her through blurred vision.

"I'll see you tomorrow," she said.

She found Mark, sitting in the dusty prop-room of the theatre, sipping coffee from a polystyrene cup.

"Okay," she said, sitting beside him on an up-turned beer-crate, "tell big sister all about it."

He didn't look up. "She's engaged," he groaned.

"Sorry?"

"Becky. She's engaged."

Natasha froze as the realization knocked her for six. So they weren't just rehearsing together.

"Can you believe that?" he asked.

"I had no idea..."

"Why didn't she tell me?" he said. "Why didn't she say?"

"Oh, Mark," Natasha sighed, sympathetically. "I'm sorry."

"And he's coming to Brighton to join her," he added.

He looked up at Natasha and she saw the tears rolling down his cheeks. "I knew it was too good to be true," he said.

She went to him and, kneeling at his feet, she

wrapped her arms around him and took his head on to her chest.

"It's not just the rejection," he said. "It's more than that. I can see now that she was leading me on all along."

"Oh, I wouldn't think so, Mark. Surely not."

Natasha's head was spinning. She felt so angry with herself for being so naive. Why hadn't she seen what was going on? She'd had no idea. Absolutely no idea! She was angry and confused and deeply distressed.

"She knows all about me," Mark went on. "And that's why she was trying to get close to me. I wanted to keep it secret…"

"Keep *what* secret?" asked Natasha.

"…but she's known all along!"

"Known what, Mark? What does she know?"

He leaned back and looked straight into her eyes.

"Let's help unload the lorry," he said.

"What secret, Mark?"

He sighed.

He's not going to tell me, thought Natasha. Suddenly she was struck with jealousy. She didn't want Becky Masters knowing more about Mark than she did. They'd only been working together for a very short time, but already Natasha felt really close to him. And she wanted to get even closer. But how could she, if there was some great secret standing in the way of their friendship?

"Let's unload the lorry," he suggested. "Then let's sort out the props for the Tech."

"And then…?"

"Then we'll go back to the digs and I'll tell you everything," he said.

As Natasha put the kettle on to boil, the landlord popped his head around the kitchen door.

"Earl Grey's gone but Glen Fiddich's in the lounge, if you're interested." He saw the glum expression on Mark's face. "Whoops," he said. "Not a good time, eh?"

"He's a bit upset," explained Natasha.

"Girlfriend trouble?"

"You could say that." Mark forced a smile.

"Then Mr Fiddich isn't right for you at this precise moment." He winked at Natasha and left.

Natasha closed the kitchen door. "Who's Glen Fiddich?" she asked.

"It's a brand of whisky," grinned Mark. "He really is crackers," he added with a laugh.

"Well ... it's nice to see your cheery smile again," she said. She gently stroked his hair. "So ... tell me about it," she added. "Warts and all."

He revealed the truth ... which astounded her.

"Mark Fallon's my stage name," he said. "My real name is Mark Leighson."

Natasha looked at him, blankly. "So?"

He smiled. "Have you read the novel of *A Stranger Love*?"

"Of course." She couldn't think where he was leading.

"So who wrote it?"

She shrugged. "Can't remember. Er ... Mary-anne someone, wasn't it?"

"Yes." He paused and took a deep breath.

"Maryanne Leighson."

"That's right." She gasped. "Your mother?"

"Not quite." He laughed. "My father."

"Oh … I see," she said, grinning from ear to ear. "Your father uses the name Maryanne Leighson when he writes."

"Only when he's writing romantic fiction," he explained. "His publisher feels that romantic fiction sells better when written by women."

"That's a bit…"

Mark raised an eyebrow. "It works both ways, Natasha. Men can be victims too."

"But how does this affect Becky?"

"Well, my father's backing the show. He and Sam Coy … of Coy Productions … have put everything they've got into it. And obviously, somehow, Becky found out."

"But…"

"So, she made a play for me. Son of the management. She wanted to suck up to me just because of who I am."

"That's nonsense," argued Natasha. "She already had the job. Why should she want to creep to you? What can *you* do for her?"

He lowered his voice. "Can you keep this under your hat?" he asked seriously. "I mean … if this gets out…"

"I promise," she said.

"None of the actors' contracts for this show are drawn up for London. They're only contracted for this tour," he explained.

"*Mine* is," replied Natasha. "My contract is for the run of the show."

"With respect," he told her, "you're not an actress on this show. You're an ASM and understudy. If the show makes it, you *will* be going into London. And so will I."

"But the others won't?"

"That would depend. My father and Sam Coy may decide to recast after this tour."

"You mean they could sack Becky Masters?"

"And Ashley. Yes."

"My God," she gasped. "No wonder Ashley's worried."

"He *should* be worried," said Mark. "He's not good, is he?"

Natasha crossed to the billowing kettle and switched it off.

"Well!" she said. "I'd better watch my step then, hadn't I? There's a spy in the camp and I'm sharing digs with him."

Mark groaned. "Oh, please don't say that, Natasha." He crossed to her and put his arms around her waist, his sudden physical attention making her tremble. "This makes no difference to us whatsoever. We're still friends. Nothing's changed between us two, has it?"

"No, of course it hasn't," she smiled. She kissed him gently on the cheek and then pulled away from him, intent on making the coffee.

But she knew … there and then … that this had changed *everything*! Any move that she now made towards him would only appear suspicious. He'd think that she only wanted to be close to him, because of who he was.

If only he hadn't told me, she thought. If only I

70

didn't know. Now it's spoilt everything!

Still chewing on slices of toast and marmalade, and dragging their coats on as they ran, they sped through the backstreets to the theatre.

"This is a good start, isn't it!" said the stage manager, as he greeted them at the stage door. "You're half an hour late."

"Sorry," puffed Mark.

"My alarm clock didn't go off," added Natasha. "And I was supposed to wake Mark. It's my fault."

"I don't care whose fault it is," he said. "But you'd better get in there and make sure you're set up. The Tech starts in fifteen minutes."

Jonathan entered the sitting-room and found Sarah staring through the French windows to the garden.

"Is this it?" he called. "Is this what you've been expecting?"

Sarah turned and raced towards him. "Give it to me!" she said, urgently.

Becky and Ashley looked at each other across the sitting-room set.

Becky laughed when she saw Ashley waving a copy of the *Daily Mirror* at her. "What's that supposed to be?" she asked.

Ashley wasn't laughing. "I couldn't find the letter," he said.

"Stop!" called Bill Grant from the auditorium. He approached the stage. "What's wrong?"

Ashley peered through the spotlights at the director. "The letter wasn't on the prop table," he said. "So I grabbed the nearest thing."

"You should've stopped!" said Bill, sounding irritated. "This is a Tech, Ashley. If technical things go wrong, we stop and sort them out."

"Sorry," said Ashley, sheepishly, realizing that his lack of experience in live theatre was now certainly beginning to show.

"Stage management!" called Bill.

Natasha and Mark left the wings and walked on to the stage.

"Where was the letter?" asked Bill.

"It was on the prop table," said Natasha. "It still is!"

"No way!" snapped Ashley.

"I'm sorry, Ashley," argued Mark, "but it was in exactly the same place it's always been … during every rehearsal."

"It was not!" said Ashley, firmly. "I went to the usual place and it was *not* there!"

Mark glared at him.

Ashley turned to the director. "It wasn't there, Bill!"

"All right! All right!" he replied. "Mark, put the letter in the right place, please! If Ashley can't find it during that black-out, we've got real problems. The letter is essential to the plot."

"Just as you say, Bill," replied Mark, as he left the stage, tight-lipped.

Natasha followed him. "It *was* there," she whispered to Mark. "I checked it before the curtain went up."

"I know," he whispered back. "I watched the idiot groping around in the dark for it. He was in sheer panic."

72

"But why should we take the blame?" asked Natasha.

"Because he's the star," replied Mark, as a matter of fact. "And we're just the ASMs. That's why."

As the final scene came to a close and the curtain dropped, Natasha and Mark sighed with relief.

"That was dreadful," said Natasha. "There wasn't much else that could go wrong, was there?"

"And none of it was our fault," smiled Mark.

The stage manager approached them. "Well done," he said. "That was very smooth."

"Smooth?" gasped Natasha. "It was awful."

"The actors were awful," he replied. "You weren't. Stage management was perfect. Even the letter was in the right place," he smiled, adding, "I saw it there when I did my check."

"I bet we don't get an apology from Mr Outback," sneered Mark.

"I'm sure you won't," laughed the stage manager. "But now's the time to find out, Natasha."

"What do you mean?" she asked.

"He's taken the letter with him to his dressing-room," he said. "Will you go and get it and tell him he must remember to leave it on the prop table at the end of each show, please."

As she left, the stage manager winked at Mark. "Rather her than me," he said.

"Come in!" he bawled.

She entered.

Ashley was gazing into the dressing-table mirror, despondently removing his make-up with a tissue.

He stared at Natasha through the mirror.

"Total incompetence!" he hissed.

She was stunned. "Pardon?"

"Call yourself an ASM? Useless!"

She was angry. "I'm sorry, Ashley, but..."

He stood, glowering, and fired his words at her. "You'd better get it right tomorrow!" he said. "If it's not right for the dress-rehearsal tomorrow afternoon, there'll be hell to pay! And God help you if anything goes wrong tomorrow *night,* lady!"

Natasha burst into tears, grabbed the letter from his dressing-table and fled from the room.

8

Ashley couldn't sleep. He turned over, switched on the bedside-lamp, reached out for his watch and noted that it was one o'clock. His heart had been racing ever since he'd lain his head on the pillow and had begun to think about tomorrow's first night of *A Stranger Love*. Everyone had said how much he'd improved over the weeks and Bill Grant had been very encouraging about the show after the Tech run. But still Ashley wasn't sure. He was sure of only one thing: that Becky Masters would steal the show. It would be Becky who'd get all the rave notices while the critics, he was sure, would condemn him as yet another Australian soap star taking work from unemployed British actors.

He climbed out of bed, slipped on his jeans and tee-shirt, pulled on his trainers and flung his denim jacket around his shoulders. He needed to get some air. It was no good lying there all night in a state of sheer panic.

As he passed by the bar, now closed and lit by one red-glowing lamp, Becky emerged on the arm of a tall, handsome blond.

"Ashley!" she said, surprised. "I thought you'd be in bed by now."

"I was," he replied. "I couldn't sleep."

"The bar's closed," she informed him. "We should've been in bed ages ago ... but I was just telling Damien about the Tech."

The tall blond put out his hand. "That's me," he introduced himself. "Becky's fiancé."

"Oh, sorry," said Becky. "Damien, this is Ashley."

Damien grinned as he shook Ashley's hand. "Yeah, I remember you from *Outback*."

"I was just saying that the Tech was pretty disastrous," went on Becky. "No matter *what* Bill Grant said."

"The dress rehearsal'll be fine," replied Ashley, unconvincingly. "Just so long as Stage Management get their act together."

"Can't wait to see the show," smiled Damien. "I've got a great seat in the front stalls, so I'll be willing you all to do well from there."

"Thanks," said Ashley. "We'll do our best not to let you down." He winked at Becky. "Won't we?"

She giggled. "Sure will."

"Well, I'm going for a stroll along the front," concluded Ashley. "To try to clear this head."

"If I don't see you before the show," Damien called after him, "good luck. Break a leg, or whatever it is you actors say on first nights." He grinned at Becky and shook his head. "What a strange expression."

As Becky and Damien climbed the stairs to their room, Ashley hurried from the hotel lobby to the car park. A walk, he thought, might clear his head. A drive in his sports car, with the top down, the wind lashing against his face, would be better.

Mark feared that he must have overslept again. The knock hurled him from the dream, in which he and Becky Masters sat lovingly entwined on a beach at midnight, to the door at which the knocking had become more frantic.

The landlord stood there in a tent-like, brightly striped nightgown.

"What's up?" asked Mark, trying to wipe the sleep from his eyes. "What's the time?"

"It's six o'clock," yawned the landlord. "Didn't you hear the phone ringing?"

"No," said Mark. "What's up?" he repeated.

"It was your director, I think. Bill Grant?"

"Yes?"

"Could you and Natasha get to the theatre for eight, instead of ten this morning? There's a problem of some kind."

Natasha hurried from her room, wrapping a dressing-gown around her.

"What sort of problem?" she asked.

The landlord began to walk down the stairs, announcing, "Who knows? Nobody tells this poor old landlord anything. I'd better wake up Mr Kelloggs and start sizzling poor old Pinky and Perky."

Natasha looked curiously at Mark.

"Don't ask," said Mark. "I've no idea." He began to unbutton his pyjama jacket. "We'd better get ready and get into the theatre as soon as possible. Ashley's probably insisted on another Tech run."

"No easy way to say this," said Bill Grant, who was waiting for them at the stage door. "You're on, Mark!"

Mark paled. "No."

"But why?" gasped Natasha.

"Ashley's crashed his car," he told them. "Broken his leg. The imbecile!"

Despite Ashley's outburst at her, Natasha found herself protecting him. "But that's terrible, Bill. Poor Ashley."

"Poor Ashley, my eye!" snapped Bill. "Speeding along the sea front at two o'clock in the morning, when he knows he's got an opening night! Fool!"

Mark was breathing deeply, trying to calm himself down, knowing that he hadn't had enough rehearsal; that he certainly wasn't ready for a first night of a new show.

"We'd better get to Ashley's dressing-room, Mark," said Bill, putting his arm around the trembling young actor's shoulders. "Let's hope you fit his costume."

As Bill led him away, the stage manager approached Natasha. "Bad news, isn't it?"

"Very," she replied.

"It's not going to be easy for you, Natasha," he said, kindly. "You'll have to take over all Mark's ASM duties, as well as managing your own."

Natasha's head was suddenly filled with images of misplaced ashtrays and wrongly-set candle-sticks.

"Can we run through it all now?" she asked. "Before the dress-run?"

"Of course." He took her hand. "Don't worry. Between us, we'll get this show on the road."

"We'll have to cancel!" shrieked Becky as she raced into the theatre, accompanied by Damien.

"We can't cancel!" glowered Bill. "It's a full house. Mark's going on."

"Don't be ridiculous!" she shouted, hysterically. "I'm not doing an opening night with the understudy!"

Bill spoke calmly. "Yes, you are, darling. Mark will be just fine ... so long as we all pull together and help him through it."

Becky flounced off to her dressing-room in floods of tears, followed sheepishly by her handsome, blond partner.

"Are you all right?" Natasha asked, popping her head around Mark's dressing-room door.

He smiled at her. "I'm not sure. I'm terrified."

"You'll be okay," she said, comfortingly.

He stood. "Does the cozzie look okay?"

She nodded, approvingly. "You wear it better than Ashley did."

"Are *you* going to be all right?" he asked her. "How are you going to cope with it all on your own?"

"Don't you even *think* about me," she gently scolded him. "Just concentrate on your performance. You're going to be wonderful."

*   *   *

Becky greeted Mark coolly as they both sat on the chaise-longue, waiting for the curtain to rise on the dress rehearsal.

"This is a bit of a shock, isn't it?" he said.

She whispered. "It's ridiculous. They should've cancelled the show."

He was hurt. "Well, thanks for your encouragement, Becky."

"You've not had enough rehearsal," she hissed. "You're not up to standard, Mark. It's impossible."

He sneered. "It seems I'm not up to standard in anything I do, as far as you're concerned!"

She tried to hush him. "Sshh. Damien's in the wings."

"It wasn't just Ashley I was understudying, was it?" he said, bitterly.

She looked away from him. "I don't know what you're talking about."

"Look, Becky," he said, determinedly. "I'm going to give this dress-run everything I've got. And I'd appreciate it if you did the same."

She turned on him. "You are *not* the director!" she said. "And even though your daddy is part of the management, you're not telling me how to behave. I'm a professional, Mark. Through and through! And even though I believe it's absurd to open this show with a poorly rehearsed understudy, I will *of course*, do my very best to make you look good!"

The curtain rose.

"So how long will you be away?" she said, immediately.

*   *   *

The actors sat in the auditorium as Bill Grant gave them notes on their performances.

"Well done, Mark," he said. "You'll be just fine tonight. Enjoy it, eh?"

"He went too far upstage on the letter scene!" said Becky. "I had to turn right round to speak to him."

"Yes. I'm sorry about that," replied Mark, quickly. "I realized as soon as I'd done it. It won't happen tonight."

"So," concluded Bill. "Well done, all. And I'd like to say a special thanks to stage management. I know what difficulties they must be going through, but from the front, you'd never have known it."

Natasha glowed with pride.

Mark winked at her.

"So ... go and have something to eat, boys and girls," said Bill. "And then let's give these first-nighters a show they won't forget. Break a leg!" He grinned. "But not literally, please."

They all laughed and returned to their dressing-rooms, bubbling with first night excitement and nerves.

"I've checked and double-checked everything," Natasha told the stage manager. "Can I dash out for half an hour? I'd like to get Mark a good luck card."

He looked at his watch. It was six-thirty. "Of course," he said. "But make it twenty minutes, eh, Natasha?"

She returned fifteen minutes later with a card

and a rose wrapped in greeting paper and knocked on Mark's door.

"All the best, Mark," she said, warmly.

He crossed the room and put his arms around her, holding her tightly. "Thanks, Natasha."

She felt comfortable being so close to him. It felt so right. She snuggled her head to his chest.

"Is your dad coming?" she whispered.

"Yes. He's already here. He's just been in to see me. I think he's more nervous than I am. Bill's taken him off for a drink to calm him down."

Natasha looked up into his eyes. "I'll be with you all the way tonight, you know that, don't you?"

The thrill of holding her suddenly and surprisingly surged through his body, making him tremble from head to foot.

"You're shaking," she said. "God, you *are* nervous."

He wanted to say, yes I'm nervous. But that's not why I'm trembling. It's because…! But he was aware that Natasha thought of him as nothing more than a friend. A *good* friend. But *just* a friend.

"Thanks for the rose," he said. "That was a lovely thought, Natasha. I don't know what I'd do without you."

She reluctantly drew away from him. "I'd better get to the prompt corner and start preparing for your star performance," she said. She kissed him on the cheek. "Good luck."

As she left the room, Becky arrived, carrying a huge bouquet of flowers and a bottle of champagne.

"Is he in there?" she asked Natasha, although

hardly looking at her.

"Yes."

Becky burst into the room.

"Darling!" she shouted. "Some flowers and a drinkie for afterwards. To wish you all the very very best!"

Mark was stunned into silence.

Natasha slunk away to her prompt corner.

"I'm sorry about this afternoon," babbled Becky. "Nerves and all that. I'm sure you understand."

"Of course," replied Mark, softly.

"You're going to be absolutely marvellous, darling," she enthused. And then, adding as what appeared to be an afterthought, she said, "Oh, by the way. I've just seen your father talking to Bill and Sam Coy."

She put down the bouquet on top of Natasha's rose and placed the champagne beside it. Then approaching her new co-star … she firmly planted a kiss on Mark's lips.

He took a step back. "Where's your fiancé?" he asked, nervously.

"Damien?"

"Yes."

"He's making himself at home in my dressing-room," she smiled.

"Then don't keep him waiting," said Mark.

9

Natasha, having a few spare minutes between her stage management duties, watched with interest and great pride from the wings as Mark joined Becky in the reprise of the title song ... *A Stranger Love:*

Aching hearts are breaking; caring
For nothing around me, while I'm sharing
A stranger's love

And though you mean the world to me;
To the world there could never be
A stranger love.

And Mark held Becky tightly in his arms.

JONATHAN: I love you, Sarah.

SARAH: And I love you.

They kissed ... as the curtain fell to thunderous applause from a packed theatre. Natasha applauded too, leaping up and down and whooping loudly, and she couldn't wait to tell Mark what a magnificent performance he'd given. The full company took four curtain calls before surrounding Mark, and heaping praise upon him.

"Where are you going, Natasha?" the stage manager asked her.

"I won't be long," she replied. "I'm just going to Mark's dressing-room to congratulate him."

"Props cleared first, please!" he commanded.

Natasha sighed deeply and hurriedly walked on to the set to remove the ashtrays, photo frames and candlesticks.

When she finally reached the passageway leading to Mark's dressing-room, she found it blocked with excited people all chattering on about the wonderful Mark Fallon.

His door was open and she could just see, above the heads of the throng, Mark's wide smile, as he thanked everyone for coming. A champagne cork popped from its bottle and everyone cheered.

"Brilliant, Mark," screeched a voice above the rattle-babble of other voices. Natasha recognized it as Becky's. "There wasn't one sticky moment from the time the curtain went up. You were absolutely brilliant, darling!"

"Too right!" shouted a man's voice, topping the din. "Well done!"

"Thanks!" Mark smiled at his proud father.

Natasha slunk back to the prop table, feeling totally spare to the celebrations.

The stage manager laughed when he saw her lining up the next day's props on the table.

"I didn't mean you had to do all that, Natasha," he said, sympathetically. "You can finish the job in the morning."

"I'd rather do it now," she replied, "if that's all right?"

He shrugged. "Please yourself. But I'm going for a pint," he said as he headed for the stage door.

Natasha took her time, one ear continuously cocked in the direction of the dressing-rooms. Bit by bit, the noise subsided and, confident that she'd now find Mark alone, she returned to his room and knocked.

There was no reply.

She tried the door handle. The room was locked.

She gasped, audibly. He surely wouldn't have left without her?

Grabbing her coat from the stage manager's office, she rushed to the stage door.

"Mark hasn't gone, has he?" she asked the door-keeper, fearing the reply.

"He's just left with a large group of people, Natasha," he informed her. "They're all going to a restaurant for a celebratory nosh-up."

He saw the look on her face.

"Yeah, I know." He raised his eyes to heaven. "Didn't ask me neither."

She walked sadly into the chill night air and made her way to the digs.

How stupid, she reprimanded herself. Why should he have even thought of you tonight? Tonight of all nights? You're just his friend, Natasha. That's all. And you should be delighted that he's left all this ASM drudgery behind him and moved up to star status.

She felt her throat tightening and desperately wanted to howl out, But I want to be with you on your big night, Mark! I love you. She stopped walking. Trembling, she stood in a shop doorway. Is that what she really felt? Did she feel that seriously about him? It couldn't be love. Not so soon, surely? She didn't know. All she knew was that she now thought about him every minute of every day; that she wanted to be with him all the time. And the thought that he would be sitting in some restaurant beside *her* ... beside Becky Masters ... made her stomach lurch. She would definitely lose him to her now. Now that he was the star of the show, she'd definitely lose him to her.

She calmed down and continued on her way home. How could she have expected anything else? If only she'd plucked up the courage to tell him of her feelings before Ashley's ghastly accident, then things might have been different. But it was too late now. Mark had no idea how she felt about him. And it was pretty obvious that they were destined to be no more than friends. That's if he still managed to find time ... now that he'd entered the big league.

She fumbled for her key and opened the door. The hallway was cosily lit. Welcoming. But she felt strange being here without Mark. She slumped against the wall, bit hard on her lip and dragged the crumpled kleenex from her coat pocket.

"Now, now, now, Cherub-face!" said the landlord, kindly, as he emerged from his lounge. "What's this all about, eh?"

Natasha couldn't speak. His comforting voice turned her gentle crying into great sobs of despair.

He went to her and put his arm around her. "Darling-heart!" he pleaded with her. "It can't be that bad, surely? Come and tell me all about it." He led her, still weeping, into the lounge and sat her in the largest of the armchairs. He sat at her feet and gently lifted her chin with his hand. "Your eyes'll go all puffy," he warned her. "There's you, as beautiful as a young Marilyn Monroe and you'll end up looking like E.T. if you carry on with all that lash-wetting ... you take my word for it!"

She laughed, gently.

"There, that's better, Angel. Now tell me," he said.

She dried her eyes and forced a smile. "It's all so daft really," she tried to explain.

"Well, it *was* his big night," he said. "All announced on the local radio, it was too. I was going to come, but I had such a lot to do here." He paused for a breath. "How was he?"

"Brilliant," she replied.

"But that's not what's upset you."

"No."

"No. I know. But it *was* his big night," he repeated. "Went off somewhere, did he? Without you?"

Tears started to well again. "To a restaurant."

"*Dragged* off, probably. Got carried away with all the excitement of the evening and allowed himself to get dragged off somewhere by the director. It always happens."

"Does it?" she asked hopefully, wondering if she were clutching at straws.

"All the time."

"I didn't even get a chance to congratulate him," she whimpered.

"You will!" he assured her. "He'll get to that restaurant, expecting you to be there. I'll bet you! And when he discovers that you're missing … he'll be so upset … he'll come straight home. Trust Roger. He knows."

She eyed him, quizzically. "Who's Roger?"

He laughed. "Me, you fool." He stood. "Now, too late for Earl Grey to visit. So, it'll have to be Glenn Fiddich."

"Oh! Not for me, thanks," she said urgently.

"I didn't mean for you," he replied. "I meant for *me*. Yours is a tiny little Man from Del Monte, am I right?"

She stared at him, blankly.

"A small orange juice!" he explained.

She smiled. "Thanks, Roger. That'd be lovely."

The actors congregated at El Pescador, a large fish restaurant on the sea front. It was nearing eleven-thirty, and the Maitre d' would usually, by now, be hurrying his final diners through their coffees and out on to the pavement. But having been fore-warned by telephone of a late and very large party of theatricals, he'd asked his staff to stay on for an hour or so. He couldn't turn down such a prestigious booking. And on seeing the glamorous and famous Becky Masters among the gathering, he was pleased he hadn't. Several long tables were pushed together to allow all the artistes to sit as one. Mark was placed at the top of the table, flanked by his father and Sam Coy. Nearby was Becky Masters, dressed up to the nines, accompanied by her blond boyfriend, Damien.

Bill Grant arrived a little later than Mark and looked for a suitable seat.

"Here, Bill!" called Sam Coy, who dragged up a chair between him and Mark.

Mark expected Natasha to follow soon after Bill. She and the stage manager were obviously still setting tomorrow's props, though he wondered why, just for once, it couldn't have been left until the following morning. He kept his eye on the door, while perusing the menu, determined that when she arrived, he'd find her a seat at the top of the table with him.

A diner on the far side of the restaurant crossed to Mark's table. "Excuse me," he said.

Mark looked up.

"My wife and I were in tonight," the man went on.

"I'm sorry?"

"We came to the show," he continued. "We weren't going to come because neither of us can stand that dreadful Ashley Gibson, but when we heard on the local news about his crash we thought we'd come along. After all, we knew the understudy had to be better than him."

Mark wasn't sure how to reply.

His father helped him out. "And did you enjoy it?" he asked.

"It was fantastic," he replied. "And you were out of this world."

"Thanks," said Mark.

"And you looked very handsome up there on stage. A real hero."

"Thanks," repeated Mark.

"It's amazing, isn't it," he went on, "what make-up and lights and things can do."

Mark laughed at his unintentional rudeness.

"Anyway, will you sign my menu?" he added. "The waiter said I can keep it."

He thrust the menu and a pen in front of Mark, who signed.

"Thank you," said the satisfied punter, who then turned his attention to Becky Masters.

"We love your sitcom on the telly," he said, "and we thought you were quite good tonight."

Mark left the table. "Excuse me a minute," he said to his father and Sam Coy as he headed for the door.

"The toilets are downstairs, sir," called an alert waiter.

"It's okay, thanks," replied Mark. "I'm just looking for someone."

He stood in the restaurant porch, peering along the promenade to see if she was approaching. He could see no sign of her.

On his way back to the table, he passed Becky, who was on her way to the Ladies.

"Anything wrong, Mark?"

He didn't want to let her know. "No. No, everything's fine."

She whispered, trying to make her words sound confidential. "You really were magnificent," she said.

She put her hand on his and he looked across

her shoulder at Damien, whose eyes were burning into him.

Mark felt his neck go hot and was afraid he might blush.

"Thanks," he croaked, nervously.

"I knew you would be," she went on. She raised her hand to his chest and rubbed it, affectionately. "And do you know," she said, "I haven't even given you a congratulatory kiss, have I?"

"And I wouldn't, Becky," warned Mark, quietly. "Damien's looking daggers at us."

"Let him look," she giggled. "He's got to get used to it. We actors kiss each other all the time. It doesn't mean anything, does it?"

"Well..." And still he kept his eye on the now fuming Damien.

"I mean, we're just friends, aren't we, Mark?" she said, gently stroking his cheek with the palm of her hand.

Damien stood.

"Becky!" hissed Mark. "Please. I don't want any trouble. Especially not tonight."

Whether his father had seen what was going on, or whether it was by pure chance, Mark had no idea, but suddenly Maryanne Leighson, alias *Mark* Leighson, banged heavily on the table with a spoon.

The gathered diners fell silent. Damien remained where he stood and Becky and Mark turned to face the smiling and now extremely successful romantic novelist before them.

"Friends," he announced. "For those who don't know me, let me explain that it is *I* who wrote the book of this wonderful musical you've all performed so brilliantly tonight."

Everyone applauded.

"And I want, if I may, to get something off my chest!"

They all listened, curiously.

"I've always despised nepotism!" he stated, seriously. "I don't believe in jobs for the boys … and I certainly don't believe in jobs for the family."

"Hear, hear," shouted one of the actors.

"But," he continued, "Bill here employed an unknown lad straight from drama school to work as an ASM and understudy on *A Stranger Love*. Call it coincidence, call it fate … or call it, if you will, an unlikely plot to one of my slushy, romantic novels!" He laughed. "But … that unknown lad, Mark Fallon – who showed us all tonight that he is, without doubt, a star in the making – just happens to be … my son!"

The actors gasped as one. They then burst into spontaneous applause.

Mark blushed and returned to his father's side. "How embarrassing!" he whispered to his father as the applause continued.

"They may as well know now, boy," said Bill Grant. "It would look bad if it got out later. There'd be all sorts of back-biting."

The waiter arrived at the table, note-pad in hand.

"Are you ready to order, gentlemen?" he asked.

"Start from the other end of the table," said Bill. "I'm sure the chorus is famished."

"Bill?" Mark asked, growing a little suspicious,

"I take it that everyone from the show was invited here tonight?"

Bill was suddenly seized by panic. He realized at that very moment what he'd done ... or rather omitted to do.

"Oh, no!" he sighed.

"You've forgotten the stage management, haven't you?"

"Yes," he replied, guiltily. "How awful."

Mark stood. "I've got to go," he said.

His father grabbed his jacket. "Don't be silly, Mark. Sit down. You can't leave now."

"I'm sorry, Dad," he said, pathetically. "But I have to. I can't leave Natasha like that. She'll think I've forgotten her."

His father grinned. "Natasha?"

"Yes."

"The other understudy," explained Bill.

"She's more than just the other understudy," said Mark. "She's my friend, Dad. And I want to be with her."

His father winked at him. "Go on, son. You go if it's that important."

Mark smiled. "Thanks, Dad."

"Thank *you*, Mark," he said. "Thanks for holding my show together tonight. I'm very proud of you. Now ... off you go to your ... *friend*." He laughed.

"See you tomorrow," said Mark, as he dashed towards the door.

10

"So, what's been going on?" asked Damien as he and Becky walked back to the hotel. "*Something* has. I can tell by the way you were looking at him."

"Don't be ridiculous!" she replied. "I was just admiring the way he handled the situation tonight. That's all. It can't have been easy, taking over from Ashley at short notice."

"That's his job!" snapped Damien. "That's what he's paid for."

"That's not the point."

"And I don't like the way he kisses you," he said.

She stopped walking and stared at him. "What? When?"

"On stage. He really seems to be enjoying it."

She laughed. "You've got to be joking?" she gasped, incredulously.

He turned on her. "I don't find it funny, Becky. I'm quite serious."

Suddenly, so was *she*. "Then perhaps we should call it a day," she hissed.

He was shocked.

"If you're going to behave like a moron," she added, "then I can't see any point in us carrying on."

"You can't mean that?"

"I'm an actress, Damien. And if I play a love scene, it has to look real. That's what acting's all about. It's not the same as accountancy. *You* don't have to get emotionally involved with your job. *I* do!"

"So, you are emotionally involved with him!" he said.

"Not with him, idiot!" she sparked. "With the part I'm playing."

He warned her, almost in a whisper, "If I ever find out you're taking me for a fool I'll..."

She felt frightened by his unqualified threat. And it wasn't for the first time in their relationship.

He began to walk quickly on.

She summoned a smile and chased after him.

"Damien, please!" she begged. "Don't be silly. There's nothing. I promise you. There's absolutely nothing between Mark Fallon and me. You do believe me, don't you?"

Without replying, he reluctantly put his arm around her shoulder ... and they continued, silently, towards the hotel.

Mark opened the street door and saw the light spilling from the lounge.

"Natasha?" he said.

"In here!" boomed Roger's voice. "Celebrating

your success with her landlord!"

Mark, shame-facedly, entered the lounge and giving a big shrug to them both, he said, "Crossed wires. I'm sorry."

Natasha beamed at him. "What for?"

"*You* know what for, don't you?" Roger jokingly scolded him.

"I thought you'd be coming to the restaurant," said Mark. "Bill's very upset that he forgot to invite you."

"It's okay," said Natasha. "Really."

Roger winked at her, trying to keep a serious face, "No, it's not. You're absolutely furious!"

"You should have stayed at the restaurant, Mark," she said, softly. "You couldn't have had time to eat."

"Have *you* eaten?" he asked her.

"No."

"So eat!" yelled Roger with a giggle.

Mark smiled at him. "Stop interfering." He put his hand out to Natasha to pull her up from the armchair. "Come on," he said. "Let's go for our own celebratory meal."

Most of the restaurants on the sea front were closed. They bought a bag of chips between them from a just-closing fish shop, and took it down to the beach. Crunching along the pebbles until they found a comfortable spot, lit only by the moon, they sat and ate.

"Was your father pleased?" asked Natasha, as her hand dived into the bag for a lukewarm chip.

"Yes. Very."

"I thought you were wonderful," she said.

His heart skipped a beat. Her approval meant as much as his father's.

She hesitated before asking, "What about your mother?"

"What about her?"

"I mean … is she coming? Are she and your father…?"

"They're divorced," he said. "But they're still friends."

"So she will be coming to the show?"

"I doubt it," he said. "She lives in Spain with her new husband."

"Oh. So you don't see her much then?"

"I go over a couple of times a year," he said. "I love it there. So will you when you see it."

She hoped she hadn't misheard. "Pardon?"

"I'll take you with me when I next go," he said. "If you want to, that is."

She wondered if this was just an idle promise. "I'd love to. I've never been abroad."

He was surprised. "Really?"

"I saved to go on a school journey once, but then it was cancelled because there weren't enough people going. I'd love to be able to sit on a warm, sandy beach somewhere."

"Like this one?" he laughed.

She felt the sharp pebbles digging into her as she reached across to him for another chip. "Hardly!"

"I quite like this, actually," he said. He looked up at the clear, almost full moon. "It's very romantic, isn't it?"

"If you're with someone you want to be romantic with, yes," she replied.

"Not that either of us are," he whispered. "Are we?"

Natasha was silent. She wanted to put out her hand to touch him; to tell him she *was* with someone she wanted to be romantic with ... that her heart was racing faster than she'd ever thought possible. But she *couldn't* reach out to touch him. She reached instead for another chip.

Mark took her silence for rejection. He was resigned to the fact that all they'd ever be ... was friends. But still he couldn't stop the longing ... the aching inside.

"And talking of romance," she said finally. "How was Becky tonight?"

"At the restaurant?"

"Yes. I assume she was there."

"With her tall, blond boyfriend. Damien."

"Oh." She immediately felt sorry she'd asked.

"It was okay," he said. "It doesn't bother me anymore. I can see quite clearly now what she was after. There's no doubt in my mind whatsoever. She'd never have gone for me if it wasn't for my connection with the management. Damien's very good looking. What could she possibly see in me, apart from a step on the ladder to more work ... more success for her career?"

"You underestimate yourself," said Natasha. "You're very attractive, Mark."

He wondered for just a second. Could it be that...? No, of course not. She was just being kind. It was typical of her. God, he wished he could tell her that the main reason Becky now meant nothing at all to him … was because he'd fallen head over heels in love. But if he told her that, she'd only laugh at the suggestion. It might even push her away from him … and *that* he couldn't bear.

"Finished with these chips?" he asked.

"Yes."

He screwed up the chip bag with one hand and with the other, he reached out and touched her arm. She stiffened under the touch. She willed him to lean across and kiss her. They sat, silently, for minutes, listening to the waves lapping on to the shore. He shuffled closer towards her.

"Natasha?" he said softly.

She gulped. "Yes?"

"There's another show tomorrow. I think we'd better go home."

He'd hardly slept all night, thinking about her, lying there in the next room, knowing he'd have to block out these feelings for her, before it totally screwed him up.

She'd slept quite soundly, but her dreams were all of him and her, lying on a Spanish beach together … with him holding her, kissing her, telling her that he loved her.

"It's about time you two came and met Sunny Side Up and his Danish friend!" called Roger from the bottom of the stairs.

Natasha and Mark took this to mean that their bacon and eggs were in the pan and they hurriedly left their rooms, almost bumping into each other on the landing.

"Morning!" yawned Natasha. "Did you sleep well?"

"Like a log!" he lied. "You?"

"Yes," she smiled. "Strange dreams, though."

As they entered the dining room, Roger emerged from the kitchen carrying two plates of eggs and bacon.

"Good morning, little ones!" he beamed. "I thought I'd make sure you were up nice and early as I realized that you'd have a lot to do today. And as you've got a show tonight, I'm sure they'll relax the hospital visiting rules … and let you see him this morning."

"Hospital?" asked Natasha.

"Ashley Gibson, of course," Roger replied. "You'll obviously be going to see him today."

"Well, I…"

Mark nudged her. "Yes. Yes of course we are," he said.

Neither had thought about going to the hospital, but Roger had laid the guilt on with a trowel. Of course they should see him. Though they weren't sure of the reception they'd receive.

"I don't believe it!" yelled Ashley, excitedly, as soon as the two of them entered the ward. "So somebody connected with that damn show does care!"

Natasha approached the bed. Mark stood a little distance off.

"Of course we care," said Natasha as she kissed him on the cheek. "How are you feeling?"

"In the leg or in the heart?" he said, sounding pathetic.

"Are you in pain?" she asked.

"No. Not now. But I've got to have an operation on it. What pains me more," he went on, "is the fact that I haven't had a word from Bill Grant ... nor the management. They really are a heartless bunch of money-grabbing..."

Natasha stopped him, afraid that he might, unaware of the relationship, go on to say something even more detrimental about Mark's father.

"I'm sure they'll be in to see you," she said. "It was all hell last night, trying to get the show on."

Ashley looked the length of the bed towards Mark, who appeared as though he were hovering, ready to dash away at any moment.

"G'day, Mark!" he said. "How did it go?"

Mark moved closer. "It was okay," he replied, nervously. "I'm sorry you had to end up like this, Ashley. I really am."

"I bet you were brilliant, weren't you?" he asked.

Mark looked embarrassed. "I..."

"He was very good," cut in Natasha.

"I'm glad," said Ashley. "D'you know I was never happy with it," he continued. "In a way, I think I'm better off here. The critics would have destroyed me."

"Nonsense," smiled Natasha. "You almost destroyed yourself. You could've been killed, Ashley."

"They'll be able to patch me up in no time," he said. "With a bit of luck. Or so they say. Get me ready for the bright lights, with no signs of a limp."

"That would be great," enthused Mark. "Let's hope you're out of here before the show finishes its run."

They were silent.

Ashley whispered, very gently, "I'm sorry, Natasha. About my bawling you out, I mean."

"Forget it."

"I was all tensed up," he tried to explain. "I felt my head was about to explode with nerves. And you just happened to be there. You took the brunt of it. I'm sorry."

"All that matters," said Mark, "is that you get yourself well. And get back to work."

"I'm not coming back to the show," he said. "That's for sure. I've told my agent to let the management know I shall be unfit for the rest of the tour." He lowered his voice and told them in confidence, "Actually, it's not true. And there's even a chance I can be gotten ready for the Aussie mini-series. But, for God's sake, don't say anything, will you? If the management of *A Stranger Love* found out, they'd sue, without a doubt."

"We won't say a word," Mark assured him.

He reached out and shook Mark's hand. "Thanks, mate."

"We didn't bring you grapes or anything," said Natasha quickly. "We didn't think about it. Is there anything we can get you?"

He thought. "I wouldn't mind a couple of mags to flick through," he replied. "There's a shop on the second floor."

"What sort of magazines?" asked Mark. "I'll go and get some."

"Anything," replied Ashley. "I'll leave it up to you."

Mark left immediately. "Won't be a minute."

Ashley took Natasha's hand. "So tell me," he said. "What's he really like in the show?"

"He's unbelievable," she replied with a smile. "I don't suppose that's what you want to hear, Ashley. But he's extremely good."

"I'm pleased." He tightly squeezed her hand. "And?"

"And?"

"Well, you two are obviously getting on very well."

"Yes." She wondered what he was asking.

"How well?"

"We're good friends."

"No more than that?"

She giggled. "Why do you want to know?"

"Just curious," he said.

"I like him, Ashley."

"I thought so."

"I like him a lot, but…"

"He doesn't feel the same way."

"I don't think so."

"I think you're wrong," he reluctantly informed her. "I saw the way he was looking at you, Natasha. I think he's probably as fond of you as you are of him."

11

The management met with Bill Grant in the hired conference room of The Regent Hotel, just before lunch the following morning.

"So, tell me," said Sam Coy, seriously. "What are your thoughts? Tell me what you think and then I'll give you my opinion."

"About what?" asked Bill.

Mark Leighson Senior grinned. "I think he's talking about my boy."

Bill sipped on his glass of iced water. "What can I say? He was superb."

"Good enough to take over the role?" asked Sam, with a glint in his eye.

Bill looked at him, questioningly. "Ashley Gibson's not going to be off for the whole of the run, so…"

"His agent called this morning," Sam interrupted. "There's no way he's gonna be ready for London … even if we wanted him!"

"So we'll have to recast, surely," said Mark's

father. "As proud as I am of my son, his stage debut isn't going to pull in the audiences. We need a big star name."

"I don't agree," argued Sam. "I think Becky Masters is big enough to bring them in."

Bill shook his head. "I'm not sure."

"Look at it this way," suggested Sam. "Why don't we let him do the out-of-town run and see how the press react? We can dish out the 'a star is born' story to the tabloids and see if they pick up on it."

"Let's face it," added Mark Senior, "we may not even get into London. It's not assured. We've got a theatre ready to take us, but if the out-of-town reviews aren't smasheroos, then we may as well forget it. With Lloyd Webber bringing in another musical next month, we can't afford to take any chances."

"Well, we've started off on the right foot," laughed Sam, as he clicked open his briefcase. "Have either of you seen the Brighton local this morning?"

He took out the newspaper and threw it on to the table for the other two to read.

"I don't believe it!" shrieked Natasha. She stood outside the newsagent's, peering over Mark's shoulder as he scanned the paper for the review section. She saw the headline and knew immediately that the critic had considered the show to be a huge success. Mark's personal review couldn't have been better. He was referred to as a talented, good-looking and sexy new star.

Mark laughed. "I can sing, yes," he said. "And maybe I'm not a bad actor ... but good-looking and sexy? How did they work that one out?"

"I think it's absolutely right," Natasha assured him, although she was aware that under the spotlight, with the costume and the make-up and surrounded by a wonderful set, he did look far more handsome than he really was in the flesh. "Up there, on stage, you look stunning," she added.

"Is that a back-handed compliment, I wonder?" he smiled.

"No." She rested her chin on his shoulder, still reading the review. "I think you're *very* sexy. And I'm sure most of the women in the audience thought so, too."

He rolled up the newspaper into a baton and playfully hit her on the head with it. She giggled.

"I've promised to meet my father at the hotel," he said. "Will you come with me?"

"He won't want me there," she replied. "He'll want to be alone with you. Anyway, he doesn't know that you've told me about the family link between management and star."

"Actually, he told the whole company last night," replied Mark. "And don't call me a star, please, Natasha."

She affectionately took his arm. "But you are!"

"I'm Mark Fallon," he said, pointedly. "The same Mark Fallon today as I was yesterday. I've just had a bit of luck, that's all."

"A *lot* of luck!" she laughed.

"Enormous good fortune!"

"Like winning the pools."

"But it won't change me," he grinned, tongue in cheek.

"It'd better!" she said seriously. "The gate to fame and fortune has opened for you," she quoted from the script of *A Stranger Love*. "So hurry through it! Before it shuts again in your face!"

He smiled at her, his voice softening, his eyes becoming cloudy as he told her, "You are so…"

"So *what*?" she asked, mock-innocently, thinking … go on! Say it! Tell me I'm beautiful, like you did before you got close to *her*! She trembled. "I'm so *what*?" she asked again.

His breathing became more shallow. He wanted at that moment to tell her exactly how he felt. He wanted to reach out and pull her close to him. He wanted, so, so much to kiss those beautiful lips and to tell her that he loved her.

"You're so … daft," he said, with a wide grin. "As daft as a brush!"

"Oh, thanks." She forced herself to smile back at him.

"Come on," he said. "Let's go and meet my father." He checked his watch. "We were expected half an hour ago in the hotel bar."

"You mean, *you* were expected," she replied.

He took her hand. "He'd love to meet you. I just know he would."

She hesitated. "If you're sure I won't be in the way?"

"Of course you won't. Anyway, Becky and her boyfriend have probably cornered him by now. He'll be relieved to see us."

Natasha let go of Mark's hand. "You didn't say she'd be there."

"Becky?"

"Yes."

"Dad's staying in the same hotel," he said. "Ironic really." He laughed. "When he first tried to book, they said they were full. But then yesterday one of the rooms was unexpectedly made vacant."

"Ashley Gibson's room?"

"Right."

"So you're Natasha," he said.

As Natasha reached out her hand to shake his, he leaned forward and kissed her on the cheek.

"Mark's told me about you."

Mark shot him a dark look. "Natasha's understudying Becky," he said. "And she's been a great friend to me."

"Yes. So you said." He winked at his son, aware that Natasha would notice. "But he didn't tell me how beautiful you were," he said to Natasha.

She blushed. "Thank you."

Mark Senior turned to his son. "Isn't she, Mark?" He sighed. "Absolutely gorgeous!"

Mark grinned nervously. "She's all right," he said, hardly able to look at Natasha.

"So, how about a drink?" asked his father.

"Just an orange juice, please," replied Natasha.

"Me too," added Mark. "I've got to do another show tonight, so during the day this body's an alcohol-free zone." He laughed. "Good one that, eh?"

Mark's father crossed to the bar.

"He's nice," Natasha said.

"Be careful!" Mark warned her. "He's certainly got his eye on you. I've seen that look hundreds of times before."

"He's very handsome for his age," said Natasha, flirtatiously.

Mark looked wounded. The very thought of Natasha being more interested in his father than in him, made him squirm.

"He'd eat you for lunch," grimaced Mark. "Then he'd go and find something else for supper."

Natasha stared across the bar at the handsome writer, sensing that Mark was showing signs of jealousy. Perhaps he does care for me after all, she thought. She wondered if she should continue piling on the compliments about his father, just to watch his reaction. But Mark soon shattered her illusions.

"I'll go for a walk and leave you alone with him, if you like," he said, successfully sounding extremely cool.

"No!" she said, in panic. "Don't be silly. I'm only playing, Mark. He's not my type at all."

He grinned, relieved. His dangerous gamble had paid off.

As Mark's father returned with the drinks, they were joined by Becky Masters.

"So, it's the gathering of the stars," she said, ignoring Natasha's presence.

Noting that Damien wasn't around, Mark greeted Becky with a furtive kiss on the cheek; a kiss that Natasha would've died for.

110

"I've been left all alone again," Becky volunteered. "Damien's been called back to London on business."

Natasha hoped the disappointment didn't show too clearly on her face.

"So I was wondering if you want to rehearse this afternoon, Mark?" she asked.

Mark knew what Becky's idea of rehearsing meant.

"A good idea," said Mark's father. "Not that there's much you can improve on, going by last night's show."

"We can go through the songs," suggested Becky. "At least it'll warm up our voices for tonight."

"If you two do that," said Mark Senior, "Natasha and I can take a ride through the Sussex countryside. There are some beautiful little villages around here."

"No, I can't rehearse," Mark quickly interrupted. "Sorry, Becky ... but Natasha and I have made other arrangements for this afternoon."

"Oh!" said Becky. "I see." She gave Natasha a withering look.

"So, we'll just finish our drinks ... and then we'll have to get off, Dad, if that's okay?"

"Sure, son," he replied. He turned to Becky. "I don't suppose *you'd* like a drive through the Sussex countryside, would you?"

They strolled slowly through Brighton's narrow lanes, passing the numerous antique shops and tiny cafes.

"You don't think she'd take up his offer, do you?" asked Natasha.

Mark shrugged. "Who knows? You said yourself that he's a handsome man, and if Becky thinks he can be good for her career…"

"I'm glad you dragged me away," she said. "It was very gallant of you!" She laughed, loudly. "A real gentleman."

He playfully punched her arm. "I just didn't want to spend the afternoon with her, that's all."

"So you feel absolutely nothing for her now?" she asked, hopefully.

"Nothing at all." He sighed. "It was all so stupid really," he went on. "I suppose I was flattered. You know, the young understudy being fancied by the TV star, and all that. Plus the fact that I felt sorry for her."

"Sorry for her?" Natasha was surprised. "Whatever for?"

"She dished me some story at that party in Fulham," he said. "About her ex-boyfriend who kept bothering her and was threatening her with violence if she didn't go back to him."

"But now you think there wasn't an ex-boyfriend?"

"Well, if there was," said Mark, "why didn't she get Damien to sort him out? He's a big, powerful-looking bloke. I'm sure he'd soon put one on anyone who was bothering her. Why did she have to come to me?"

"Unless Damien *was* the ex-boyfriend!" suggested Natasha.

Mark stopped walking and turned to face her, surprised. "You don't think so?"

"I don't know. It's possible, isn't it?"

"Yes," he said. "Of course it is. It didn't even cross my mind."

Natasha noted that they were standing outside a small terraced house with a sign in the window. She grabbed the opportunity to change the subject, not wanting to spend the whole afternoon discussing the love-life of Becky Masters.

"Have you got any cash on you?" she asked.

"A bit. Why?"

She turned him round to face the sign.

"It's a fortune-teller," he said.

"Shall we go in?"

"Whatever for?" he laughed. "You don't believe in that old rubbish?"

She didn't reply.

He was astounded. "You don't, surely?"

"Let's go in," she pleaded. "I've never been to one before, and I've always wanted to."

He sighed, took her hand, pushed open the door and gently led her into the darkened hallway.

Mrs Lee, so the photos on the wall informed them, had told the fortune of almost everyone in show business.

"Yeah, they've all been through 'ere, ducks," she said to Natasha in a strong East London accent. "I've 'ad everyone from dear old Benny Hill to..." she whispered confidentially while looking around the room for imaginary spies... "let's just say ... members of royalty."

Mark raised his eyebrows in disbelief. This woman was a cliché of every TV comedy clairvoyant he'd ever seen.

She immediately noted the expression on his face.

"It's no good you coming to me if you're gonna sit there all cynical," she snapped. "If you start off like that, there's no point. So perhaps you'd better go and sit in the back room while I do a reading for your girlfriend."

Any tiny beliefs that Mark *may* have had, had certainly disappeared now. If this woman thought that Natasha was his girlfriend ... what other nonsense was she likely to come up with?

"Yes, perhaps I *will* wait outside," he said, not unkindly, hoping that he'd be out of earshot before the clichéd Mrs Lee came up with the line, "You can cross my palm with silver."

Natasha entered the back room some thirty minutes later, followed by Mrs Lee.

"Your turn, Mark," she said.

Mark smiled warmly at Mrs Lee. "I don't think so," he said.

"So you don't want to know if the show's going to run?" she asked.

Mark looked at Natasha, sure that she must have discussed *A Stranger Love* with the fortune-teller.

Natasha's mouth dropped open. "I haven't said a word," she said to Mark. She stared at Mrs Lee. "How did you...?"

"Know?" laughed Mrs Lee. "It's my job, ducks."

Mark reluctantly followed Mrs Lee into the front room and sat opposite her at the dining table, gazing doubtfully at the crystal ball between them.

They sat silently for minutes, the sound of Mrs Lee's wheezing chest making him feel extremely uncomfortable. Mark wondered if he should gaze into the ball and then tell the woman that he could see clearly that she was a two-packets-of-fags-a-day-lady. The idea amused him.

But only momentarily.

She glared at him, accusingly, from across the table.

"I've got asthma," she said, sharply. "I don't smoke."

Mark gulped and felt the palms of his hands begin to sweat.

He listened intently to what the woman had to say. She told him that he'd been suddenly thrust into the limelight of showbiz and that he should make the most of it while it lasted, because as we all know … fame and fortune are only passing things. What was more important, she told him, was a new-found personal relationship which would grow stronger and stronger. And that if, in the next few weeks, he were to grab the opportunity offered to him … it would change his life completely.

As Mark and Natasha stepped from the house into the bright sunlight beaming down on to The Lanes, both were silent.

They walked towards the promenade and as they crossed the busy road to the beach, Mark gently took Natasha's hand.

"Stupid, wasn't it?" he said, softly.

*   *   *

Mrs Lee switched on the kettle to make herself a cup of tea. She was pleased about that one. Nice couple. Obviously desperately in love. When she'd read all about the show in the local paper earlier that morning, she'd thought *then* that he was a pleasant-looking boy. Not exactly handsome. Not like some of the stars she'd met. But he wasn't *bad*-looking. And his photo certainly didn't do him credit. There was something about those eyes and that open face of his that really was quite attractive. She wished him well. She wished them both well. Yes. Nice couple.

She opened her kitchen cabinet and took out a packet of tea bags. Then she reached for her pack of cigarettes.

12

After such critical acclaim, the second perform-ance of *A Stranger Love* was played to a packed house. The show itself received a standing ovation, and praise from delighted stage-door Jennies was heaped upon Mark Fallon.

"It'll be different today," said Mark as he and Natasha walked into the theatre from their digs. "I bet the matinee will be full of old ladies who'll hate me."

Natasha laughed. "Nonsense. You'll be as popular with Brighton's old ladies as you were on the first night … and last night. You'll see!"

"I still have to pinch myself, you know," he said. "I really can't believe it's happened so quickly."

They reached the promenade and leaned over the rail, staring at the noon-day sunbathers on the beach.

"Will your agent be coming?" asked Natasha.

"He said he'll try to get here on Saturday," explained Mark, "but he's got two clients opening in the West End this week, so I doubt it somehow. He might get to Bournemouth next week and see it there."

Natasha's eyes squinted before the powerful sun. "What a smashing day," she sighed. "Pity we've got to spend it shut away in the theatre, isn't it?"

"We could come and have a swim between the matinee and the evening show," suggested Mark. "There's a two-hour break."

Natasha shrugged. "For the stars, yes. Not for me. I've got to re-set the props."

Mark grabbed her arm. "Why don't I help you? We can get it done quicker with two. And *then* we can come to the beach."

She drew away from him. "No way. I'm not having the star of the show helping me with my ASM duties."

She began to stroll on. He followed her.

"Natasha, don't be silly. It's got nothing to do with the star and the ASM. We're friends. And I want to be with you."

She smiled affectionately at him and walked on in silence.

At the stage door there were several cards for Mark, which he took into his dressing-room to read as Natasha made her way to the prompt-corner to begin the set-up.

The stage manager greeted her, cheerfully. "Good news, darling," he said. "We've got a new girl starting tomorrow as an ASM. So you won't have to do all this yourself."

Natasha was surprised. "A girl? I thought they'd

be hiring someone to understudy Mark."

"Jason's doing it," he told her. "That tall, red-headed boy in the chorus."

"Oh!" She sounded disappointed. She'd always found Jason to be so uncommunicative. He was the only member of the chorus who'd never spoken to her.

"You'll like him," said the stage manager. "He'll make a very good Jonathan to your Sarah, I'm sure. He's just a bit shy, that's all."

Natasha began setting out the props, in order, on the prop table before her. "So I suppose we'll be rehearsing every day in Bournemouth," she mumbled, cursing the fact that she'd be called into the theatre every day, while Mark could stroll around Bournemouth, enjoying the sunshine.

"I'm sure we'll keep rehearsals to a minimum," he replied. "After all, none of us want to be cooped up in the dark all day … least of all me."

Natasha continued with her work, wondering how it would feel to rehearse with Jason. How would she cope when it came to the kiss? It would be so strange having already rehearsed that scene with Mark and Ashley Gibson. And what would it be like with the tall, red-headed, shy Jason? And she wished so much that she were still able to rehearse with Mark.

Mark opened his cards. There was one from his agent, congratulating him on his wonderful press-notices. There was a two-day-late first night card from his mother, post-marked from Spain, and saying that she was sure he'd make a wonderful

ASM and that she hoped that he'd get the chance to play the part at some stage during the run. And there was a card from Ashley Gibson, wishing him all the best for the run of the show with sincere wishes that *A Stranger Love* would make it to London, and make Mark a big, big star. There was a postscript, the contents of which knocked Mark for six. He read it over and over again: "Not sure if you realize how much Natasha thinks of you. Don't delay! Act today!"

Mark stuck the cards on to his dressing-room mirror with some Blu-Tack and sat back in his chair, pondering on the message. How did Ashley know what Natasha felt? Had he just assumed that she was fond of him? Or had she said something to him? He was sure it must have been the former. There was no way Natasha felt any more than friendship for him. He was sure of that. Had she felt more than that, he would have known. Wouldn't he?

The matinee wasn't a full house, but the audience was obviously enjoying every minute of it. Natasha watched proudly, although somewhat jealously, from the wings as Mark held Becky in his arms.

JONATHAN: If it were the other way round, I'm not sure that I could forgive you.

SARAH: It hasn't been easy.

JONATHAN: I know. I'm sorry, Sarah. I know you'll find this difficult to believe,

but I've never stopped loving you.
Never.

SARAH: Oh, Jonathan.

As Mark kissed Becky, she appeared, from where
Natasha stood, to almost collapse in his arms. Her
hand rose sensuously up Mark's spine and she
gently caressed the back of his neck as she
responded to the kiss with such passion.

Natasha whispered to the stage manager, "She's
never done that before."

He smiled at her, unaware how Natasha felt
about Mark, "Getting carried away, if you ask me.
I think our Becky's got a soft spot for him, don't
you?"

The kiss continued for far longer than usual and
Natasha turned away to organize her next prop
setting, her heart pounding furiously.

Mark hurriedly removed his costume and make-
up and raced to the prompt-corner to find Natasha,
broom in hand, about to sweep the stage.

"Coming for some tea?" he asked.

She grinned at him. "Forgotten the swim, then?"

He shrugged. "You said you wouldn't have time.
But you have got time to go for something to eat."

She sighed. "I haven't, Mark. Sorry. If I get this
finished in time, I'll rush out for a sandwich."

He looked very disappointed. "Oh, well, I'll see
you later, then?"

"Yes, see you later."

*   *   *

He opened the stage door to be greeted by dozens of women of all ages, pushing their programmes in front of him, asking him to sign his autograph.

"You were brilliant," blurted out one grey-haired pensioner. "Took me right back to the thirties. Lovely."

"Thanks," replied Mark.

"And she was good too," said another. "That Becky Masters. I never thought she could sing like that. You two go really well together."

The gathered fans all giggled, knowingly.

Mark charmed them with his smile. "It's only acting," he said.

One fan dug another with her elbow. "Tell us another," she laughed.

Mark laughed along with her. "We're just good friends," he said.

Having signed all the programmes, he excused himself, saying he had to have a break before the evening show, and he ambled up towards the town.

"Mark!" he heard. He turned to see Becky hurrying up behind him.

"How did you get out so quickly?" he asked. "Didn't you get stopped by all those autograph hunters?"

She dismissed the comment with a flick of the wrist. "I never sign autographs."

"You didn't just ignore them, surely?"

"They don't own me," she replied. "When you've been signing autographs for as long as I have, darling, you'll wisen up. You just smile sweetly and say you're in a hurry."

He eyed her, disapprovingly. "So where are you off to now?" he asked.

"I thought we could go for something to eat," she said. "How about Browns' in The Lanes? They do a nice quiche." She slid her arm in his and led him away.

"I needed to talk," she said mysteriously, as she picked her way through her quiche and green salad.

He wondered what she had up her sleeve.

"About what?"

"About us."

He sighed. "I don't know what you're talking about."

"It isn't what you think," she said. "I know you think I was just after you, because of your father, but it wasn't like that at all. I really like you, Mark. You're…"

"I'm what?" he snapped. "Easy prey?"

"Don't!" she pleaded. "You're kind … and gentle…"

"You're engaged!" he said. "He's a good-looking bloke who's obviously in love with you. So what are you playing at?"

"*I* don't love *him,* Mark," she snivelled. Tears welled up in her eyes. "I thought I did. But I don't. He's so possessive. I can't look at another man without him going raving mad."

Mark stared at her, incredulously. "Becky, I don't know where I fit in here? It's got nothing to do with me. If you don't love him, tell him. Break off the engagement. But don't drag me into it."

"I can't tell him," she said. A tear rolled down her cheek. "He's so … it frightens me, Mark. How can I tell him I want to leave him? I don't know what he'd do."

"You've got to tell him," responded Mark. "You can't just lead the poor guy on like that. You've got to make a clean break. For both your sakes."

"So what do I do?" she begged. "Tell me. Do I just call him up and tell him that I'm dating *you*?"

Mark almost choked on his salad. "What?"

"Well, *do* I?"

He was furious. "No, you *don't*! Don't bring me into this, Becky! You and your boyfriend's tiffs have absolutely nothing to do with me. So leave me out!"

She began to sob. "But I want you, Mark."

He stood, preparing to leave. "I'm sorry about that, Becky!" he said. "But there's nothing I can do about it."

"I hope you've set my letter properly," joked Mark as he approached Natasha, who was sitting in the prompt-corner. "I don't want to take the *Daily Mirror* on by mistake."

He expected her to look at him and smile. She didn't. She nibbled on a bar of chocolate.

"That'll do you a lot of good," he went on. "Didn't you get a chance for a break?"

"Yes," she replied.

He stared at her. "What's up?"

"Nothing."

"So if you had a break, why didn't you go and get yourself something proper to eat?"

"I did. The stage manager overheard our conversation, and he said he'd finish setting up so I could go to tea with you."

He was surprised. "So why didn't you?"

"I saw all those autograph hunters at the stage door, surrounding you, so I came back here."

"But they weren't there for long," said Mark.

"I know. I came out again to see if they'd gone, and you were walking down the street, arm in arm with Becky Masters."

"Oh!"

She finished her chocolate and screwed up the wrapper. "I'd better get on, Mark. There's still some bits and pieces to do."

"It wasn't what you think," he said.

"It doesn't matter, does it, Mark?" she replied. "It doesn't matter to me what you do. It's just that you lied to me, that's all. And I don't like my friends lying to me."

He gripped her arm. "We've got to talk!" he said. "Tonight … after the show. We'll take a bottle of wine back to the digs and really talk, Natasha."

He was determined to tell her. There was no way he could possibly feel anything for Becky Masters. It was Natasha he was in love with. And she had to know. Even if it meant humiliation and rejection, he had to tell her. And he wondered, against all hopes, if Ashley Gibson was right. Would she have been quite so upset at seeing him with Becky, if she didn't feel *something* for him?

"I've got something important to tell you," he said. "Very important."

"Forget it," she replied. "I'm going out tonight.

I've been asked to a disco."

He began to tremble. "Who by?"

"Jason," she said. "That red-headed boy from the chorus. He's taking over your understudy job and I think he wants to get to know me a bit better before we start rehearsals."

"Which disco?" enquired Mark. "Not *Stars*?"

She looked up at him, quizzically. "How do you know?"

He forced a smile. "Because we're all invited. The whole company. There's an invitation in the green room, Natasha. It's a publicity ploy to boost *Stars*."

"I didn't see it," she mumbled, embarrassedly.

"You don't want to go, do you?" he asked, child-like. "Let's go home with a bottle, eh? Just you and me. We've got to talk, Natasha."

She was terrified that he might be about to tell her something that she didn't want to hear: that he'd fallen for Becky Masters but hadn't had the guts to tell her when she'd asked. And he'd probably try to tell her that of course it made no difference to *their* relationship. That they would still remain good friends.

"Isn't Becky going to the disco?" she asked, pointedly.

He sighed, deeply. "I've no idea."

"I don't think we've really got anything to talk about, Mark," she said finally. "I think I'd rather go to the disco with Jason."

"And the whole company!" he added, harshly.

"I've got work to do," she said. "Good luck with the show tonight."

She walked on to the set to double-check, with clouded eyes, that everything was in its correct place for the evening performance.

13

Stars was heaving with ravers, many of whom had come to spot TV's Becky Masters. Mark had ambled home after the show, desperately hoping that Natasha would change her mind and leave Jason and the rest of the cast at the disco. On arriving at his digs, he found Roger dashing from the kitchen to the dining-room with a huge plate of interesting-looking hors d'oeuvres.

"You're home," gasped Roger, sweating on his top lip. "I thought you'd be going to the celebrity night at the disco."

"Well, I..."

"I've got all the am-drams here after their first night of *Kiss Me Kate!*" he expostulated. "Come and greet them ... pro to am. Join us for din-dins."

Mark could think of nothing worse than spending the next few hours with the local amateur theatre group, but wasn't sure how, if he stayed in the house, he could avoid offending Roger, by not attending.

"I *am* going to the disco," he said, quickly. "I've only come home to change my shirt." He smiled at Roger. "But thanks, anyway."

"They'll be ever so disappointed," mock-pouted Roger, "but we all understand a star's priorities."

Mark opened the door to the dining-room so that Roger could pass through with the plate ... and then he quickly scurried up the stairs to his room.

Not bothering to change shirts, he lay on his bed for minutes, staring up at the ceiling, knowing that he'd have to go the disco now; or at least, find some other excuse to leave the house. He looked at his watch. It was gone eleven, and Natasha would certainly have arrived at *Stars* by now. And so would Becky!

Natasha skulked in a corner, shouting to Jason above the music pounding from the dance floor. She realized it was a ridiculous idea, to accompany him here, so that they could both get to know each other better. This just wasn't the right place. She couldn't hear a word he said. From time to time she eyed the main staircase which led down into the bar from the disco's main entrance, hoping that Mark would arrive. After their harsh words, she hadn't had time to speak to him again, and she deeply regretted her reaction to seeing him with Becky. Jealousy was an unattractive emotion and she wished that she'd kept it in check. After all, no matter what she felt for him, she knew that she couldn't bear to lose him as a friend.

She saw Becky Masters descend the steps, arm in arm with an older man.

She looked again. It was Mark's father.

"Do you want to dance?" shouted Jason above the din.

"In a minute!" she shouted back. "Shall I go and get us some drinks?"

"*I'll* go!" said Jason. "What do you want? Another beer?"

"*I'll* get them!" insisted Natasha.

She crossed to the bar and stood beside Becky and Mark senior.

Becky saw her first … and ignored her.

"Hello, Natasha!" said Mark senior. "I thought Mark said he wasn't coming!" He looked around the bar for his son, assuming he'd have arrived with Natasha.

"He *hasn't* come," replied Natasha. "I've come with Jason."

Becky spoke sharply to her. "He hasn't come?" There was panic in her voice. "Why hasn't he come?"

"I don't know," replied Natasha. "I think he must have been tired."

"I'm not tired," said a voice.

They all turned to see Mark behind them.

He took Natasha's hand. "Hi!" he said as he kissed her on the cheek. She felt her heart give a flutter.

"I'm glad you've come, boy," said his father. "You shouldn't turn down any invitations which can get publicity. The press'll be here later to take some photos." He grinned, mischievously. "So look as though you're enjoying yourself, whatever you do."

"Good evening, Mark," said Becky, plaintively. She looked at him, cow-eyed.

He gave her a broad smile and a friendly wink, before leading Natasha away into a darkened corner.

"What are you drinking?" he asked her.

"I'm getting them for Jason and me, Mark," she explained.

"I'll get them ... and join you," he smiled.

She grinned at his cheek. "You can't!" she hissed. "I've come here with Jason. You can't just come over and join us. It'll look as though it's all pre-arranged."

"You're not dating him, Natasha," he laughed. "He's only trying to get to know you for work purposes. And that's very sensible of him. But he can still get to know you if I'm around."

"How do you know I'm not dating him?" she asked.

"Because he's not interested in you in that way," he informed her. "In fact, he's much more likely to be interested in me!"

She blushed. "Oh!"

He laughed. "Why don't we have a drink or two ... and a little chat with Jason ... and then go home? I really want to talk to you, Natasha." He pleaded. "Please?"

She sighed. How could she resist him? Even though she'd seen that wink he'd given Becky. They'd obviously talked about it earlier ... he and Becky. And tonight, he'd probably informed her, "I'm going to tell Natasha exactly what's going on between us."

"Well?" he asked.

"Okay," she replied, doing her best to sound reluctant.

"Great," he said. "I'll get the drinks. What's Jason's tipple?"

Just thirty minutes later, as Mark was about to ask Natasha if she wanted to go home, Mark senior approached with Becky ... and a photographer from the *Sussex Recorder*.

"This is Mark Fallon," said Becky to the bespectacled photographer. "My co-star."

Mark tutted. "We were just leaving," he said.

His father looked at him, shaking his head. "Mark! A couple of photos first, please."

Mark turned to Natasha, who in turn, knowing she didn't want to get involved, turned away to talk to Jason.

"If we can have the two of you on the dance floor, first," suggested the photographer, "and then we'll move up to the top bar where it's more intimate."

Becky took Mark's arm and pushed through the crowd to the dance floor, ignoring the cat-calls and lewd comments from the youths who recognized the beautiful Becky Masters.

The last thing that Mark felt like doing was dancing, but, for his father's sake he threw himself into the part, pretending he was really enjoying himself. Becky was lapping up the attention from the young men, all wolf-whistling at her from the bar as she clung to Mark and danced provocatively to the pulsating rhythm blasting across the floor.

The photographer finally indicated that he'd

shot enough here … and then he pointed towards the staircase.

Becky left the dance floor, grabbing Mark's hand and dragging him on behind.

"Let's go up to the quiet bar!" she shouted above the noise.

Mark let go of Becky's hand and looked across to the dark corner where Natasha was tête-à-tête with Jason. Natasha hadn't seen the two of them, followed by the photographer and Mark's father, climb the stairs. Jason *had* seen them and appeared to disapprove.

"She looks as though she's going to eat him, given half a chance," he tutted.

"Pardon?" Natasha wondered what he meant.

"Becky Masters!" he replied. "She's just gone upstairs with Mark."

Natasha tried not to react.

"I thought *you* and him were an item at one point," went on Jason. "Everyone in the company thought so."

Natasha placed her drink on a small table by the wall. "I'm not feeling too good, Jason," she said. "I think I'll go and get some air. It's so stuffy in here."

"I'll come with you," he replied, sounding concerned. "You do look a bit pale."

She kissed him on the cheek. "Thanks, Jason. But I'm okay. Honestly. I won't be long."

She made her way to the staircase.

"If you could get just a bit closer to each other," said the photographer.

The upstairs bar was empty and perfectly, moodily lit for those who wanted to smooch in private ... away from the bustling body of the disco.

Becky wrapped her arms around Mark's neck. "This better?" she asked.

Mark put his arms around her waist and acted the part of Jonathan, gazing longingly into her eyes.

"That's great," said Mark senior. "Now, how about the kiss?"

Mark suddenly withdrew from Becky's embrace. "No," he said. "Sorry."

Becky looked deeply hurt.

"Why not?" asked the photographer. "It'd look great. Perfect ad for *A Stranger Love* ... and great for *Stars* disco."

"No!" said Mark, adamantly. "If I were in costume, that'd be fine. But I'm not appearing in the paper as though Becky and I have got something going once we're out of the spotlight. I'm sorry." He turned to his father. "I think he's got enough shots," he said. "I'm going back to Natasha."

He hurried from the bar and down the stairs, leaving a distressed Becky and a petulant photographer.

Mark crossed the downstairs bar to Jason's corner.

"All done?" asked Jason.

"Yes. Where is she?" asked Mark.

"Natasha?"

"Yes."

"She went out to get some air," he explained. "I offered to go with her," he added quickly, and looking very shame-faced. "But she said she was all right."

Mark raced back across the bar, leapt the stairs two at a time and ran into the foyer. He hoped to find her here. There was no sign of her. He left the building and hurried into the street just as a cabbie was pulling away from the kerb, taking Natasha with him.

"Natasha!" he called. He ran along the street, hoping to see another cab approaching. There was none. He ran on, deciding that it would probably be quicker to run all the way to the digs than to hang around here for a passing taxi.

He arrived ten minutes later, panting and sweating and trying with trembling hand to get his key in the lock.

As he entered the hall, he heard the sound of laughter coming from the dining-room and, desperate to avoid Roger's attention, he began to creep up the stairs to his room.

He stood outside Natasha's door, sweat dripping from his forehead.

"Natasha!" he softly called. "Can I come in?"

There was no reply.

"Natasha!"

He placed his hand on her bedroom door handle and wondered if he dare go in.

He withdrew it.

"Natasha! Please!"

He put his hand back on the handle and turned it. The door was locked.

Roger's voice boomed up the stairs. "Mark? Is that you?"

Mark stammered a reply. "Yes, Roger."

"Come and join us for Brazilian Beans!" he said.

"Well ... I'm a bit tired, Roger," Mark called back. "And coffee will only keep me awake."

"As you please, Sunshine," Roger replied. "Natasha's down here though."

Mark gulped. "Oh. Well, just for a while then," he said as he hurried down the stairs.

Mark and Natasha enjoyed the company. All men. Each of them more eccentric than Roger, all telling tales of their exploits in the local amateur theatre group.

Mark sat on the only available seat; a low, hard-backed chair, from where he kept glancing across at the giggling Natasha, who appeared to be avoiding his gaze.

After a third cup of coffee, Natasha aimlessly looked at her watch and gave a little shriek.

"I don't believe it!" she said. "It's half past two!"

"Doesn't time fly," gasped Roger, "when you're having an hilarious gossip?"

"I must go to bed," said Natasha. "Or I shall be good for nothing tomorrow." She stood.

"Me too," agreed Mark. "Thanks, Roger." He bade good night to all the amateur actors and left the room, following on Natasha's heels.

As they reached the top landing, he reached out for her. "Natasha, can we talk?"

She turned to face him. "It's very late, Mark."

"Please?"

She unlocked her door. "You'd better come in," she said.

He followed her into her room and closed the door behind him.

She sat on her bed and looked up at him. "If you're going to explain all about your relationship with Becky Masters," she said, "you can forget it. I don't want to know. We can still be friends, if that's what you want, but I'm sorry, Mark ... I don't like her. And she doesn't like me. I really don't want anything to do with her."

He smiled at her and wrung his clammy hands together, nervously.

"You've got it all wrong, Natasha. Totally wrong."

She responded flatly. "Have I?"

"This isn't easy to say, Natasha, but..."

She stood. "Then don't say it."

"Do you feel anything for me?" he asked, his voice faltering.

She wondered just for one short second if she could have been mistaken.

"You *know* what I feel for you," she replied. She wanted to blurt out her true feelings, but ... "You're my friend," was all she said. "I don't know how I would have coped in this job if it wasn't for you."

"I love you, Natasha," he said quickly.

She was silent, looking at him blankly.

"I feel nothing at all for Becky Masters," he continued. "I've been trying to tell you for ages. I love you, Natasha."

She sat back on her bed. "Oh, Mark."

He was deeply embarrassed by her reaction.

She buried her face in her hands.

"I'm sorry," he rushed on, his face growing bright red. "I shouldn't have said anything." He wondered if she were crying behind those trembling hands which were hiding her face. Or had he stunned her into silence?

She slowly lowered her hands to reveal a beaming smile. "Oh, Mark," she replied. "Of course you should have said it."

He stared, incredulously, at the smile on her beautiful face. She couldn't mean...?

"Mark," she said, softly. "I feel the same way about you."

He suddenly felt as though he'd stopped breathing.

"I love you, Mark."

He went to her and placed his arms around her waist, raising her gently to her feet.

"Kiss me – " she said – "then go to bed!" She giggled. "And then you can tell me in the morning ... in front of Mr Kelloggs and dear old Pinky and Perky ... that it wasn't all a great big dream."

They both laughed.

And they held each other tightly.

So tightly.

Then he kissed her.

Gently.

And before she'd had time to open her eyes ... he'd tiptoed silently from the room.

14

Roger emerged, bleary-eyed, from the kitchen and placed the plate of bacon and eggs in front of Natasha.

"Roger's not his ebullient self today," he yawned.

She laughed. "I'm not surprised. It was a very late night."

She'd knocked earlier on Mark's door to wake him and was surprised that he wasn't already breakfasting.

"Mark's gone out," Roger informed her.

She immediately began to worry. Had he regretted what he'd said to her last night and this morning felt that he couldn't face her?

"Oh?" she said, trying to sound nonchalant.

He smiled. "Won't be long though. He's popped to the shop."

She immediately heard his key in the lock and as he stepped into the hall he called out cheerfully, "I hope Pinky and Perky are waiting for me, Roger!"

He entered the room with a carrier bag, grinning at Natasha.

"Morning," he said. He gently ruffled her blonde hair with his fingertips before taking his seat opposite her.

"And how are you this morning?" he asked her.

She smiled at him. "Fine. You?"

"Couldn't be better," he said.

"Good morning, Roger … and how are you this morning Roger?" asked Roger. "I'm fine too, Roger," replied Roger.

Mark laughed. "I've already greeted you once this morning."

"So you have," Roger replied. "I'll just go and get your breakfast, sir," he said. "I won't be long, sir." He bowed and went into the kitchen.

"So what's in the bag?" Natasha asked.

"Sarnies, tins of coke and some apples," replied Mark. "I thought, as it's such a beautiful day, we'd go for a picnic."

Natasha was thrilled. "Really? Where?"

"Out on the Downs somewhere."

"By train?"

Roger re-entered, carrying a warm plate of bacon and egg. "By taxi," he said. "It'll be here in half an hour, sir, as you requested, sir." He placed the plate in front of Mark. "Pinky and Perky with their sunny little friend," he said.

The taxi driver knew the perfect spot, a half-hour's drive from Brighton. He left them by a stile leading to a field populated with sheep, promising to call back for them at four o'clock.

"Don't let us down, will you?" Mark said as he paid him his fare. "We've got a show to do tonight."

"Of course I won't," the driver replied. He winked at Mark. "Have a nice day," he added, as he turned the car around and trundled back along the quiet country lane.

Mark climbed over the stile into the field and put his hand out, helping Natasha to follow him.

"It's like a picture book," sighed Natasha.

The field rose and fell in gentle undulation towards a small, lone, thatched cottage in the distance. The white sheep, dotting the green, began to bleat loudly as Mark and Natasha made their way across the field to a cosy hollow, backed by trees.

"Here?" asked Mark.

"Why not?"

They sat among clumps of daisies and Mark opened the carrier bag, taking out a small cloth, borrowed from Roger, which he spread on the grass before them. He carefully set out the food and then lay back, feeling the sun burning his face.

"This is the life, eh?" he said.

Natasha lay beside him, her hands behind her head. "Heaven," she replied.

They were silent for a few minutes, listening to the sheep-bleats in the distance.

Mark turned over, leaning up on one elbow, staring at the beautiful blonde at his side. He gently ran his fingertips across her forehead, pushing back the fringe of hair.

"Natasha?" he asked, almost whispering.

"Mm?"

"Did you mean what you said last night?"

She smiled; a gentle flicker of a smile ... keeping her eyes closed, enjoying his touch.

"Of course," she replied in a returned whisper. "Did you?"

He leaned across and softly brushed her lips with his.

She sighed.

He lay his arm across her and began to kiss her, more passionately now.

She reached up and stroked the back of his head, responding to his warm, tender kiss and she wished that she could stay like this for ever. No hustle and bustle of the big town ... no traffic ... no work. Just the sound of bird-song, the rustling of the trees, the gentle calling of the sheep ... and his soft, soft lips upon hers.

"Told you I wouldn't let you down, didn't I?" said the taxi driver as he pulled up at the stile to find Natasha and Mark waiting for him. "Did you have a good day?"

Mark shrugged. "It was okay," he smiled. He looked at Natasha and winked.

She giggled. "Yes, it was all right."

"This is Cyndy, the new ASM," announced the stage manager as soon as Natasha entered the stage door. He looked at his watch. "I thought I asked you to be here by three o'clock, Natasha?" he added, solemnly.

She was surprised. "No," she replied. "You didn't

say anything. I thought I had to be here at my usual call-time."

"Well, there's a lot to do," he rushed on. "I'd like you to go through scene one's prop-setting with Cyndy."

Natasha smiled at the girl; a short, waif-like youngster with cropped, fair hair and tiny round spectacles balanced on the end of her nose.

"Have you done any ASMing before?" she asked her.

"Quite a bit, yes," replied Cyndy. She grinned from ear to ear. "I'm not as young as I look. I could probably give you ten years."

Natasha looked at her more closely.

"I'm twenty-eight," said Cyndy.

"And very experienced," added the stage manager. "I've worked with Cyndy dozens of times. Just show her the settings, Natasha, and she'll pick it up straight away."

Mark appeared in the prompt-corner, in costume, just before the half-hour call.

"All set?" he asked. He put his arm around Natasha and kissed her on the cheek.

"Yes." She smiled at him. "Thanks for a lovely day, Mark."

"Thank *you*."

"We must do it more often," she laughed.

"Not in Brighton, though."

"No," she said, sadly, knowing that tomorrow was their last show here.

"Bournemouth'll have picnic spots, I'm sure," he said, confidently.

"I hope so."

"So what about tonight?" he asked. "This charity do at the Pavilion Ballroom?"

"Can't wait," she replied. She hesitated. "I … I suppose *all* the company's going?"

He knew what she meant. "Don't worry about Becky," he said. "I'm sure she's got the message at last. She'll probably keep well away from us."

"I'm Cyndy," said the new ASM suddenly, interrupting the two of them and putting out her hand to shake Mark's.

"Oh … this is Mark Fallon, Cyndy," said Natasha. "The star of the show."

"Hi, Cyndy!" said Mark. He stroked Natasha's cheek with the back of his hand. "Well, I'd better go and warm up the voice," he said. "See you after the show."

As he left, Cyndy stared after him.

"Well … he's a bit of all right, isn't he?" she sighed.

"Actually," replied Natasha, with a smile, "he's a *lot* of all right … and he's mine."

The Pavilion Ballroom was brightly lit, its white-clothed tables giving off a harsh glare under the dozen or more chandeliers.

"A bit vulgar, isn't it?" said Mark as he and Natasha sat at one of the tables facing the small, red-velvet-curtained stage.

"Are we being fed?" she whispered. "I don't see any sign of food."

Almost on cue, a waiter arrived bringing a large oval plate of thinly cut, crust-vacant sandwiches.

"We can have another picnic," grinned Mark. He

144

rubbed her arm gently with his open hand. "Give us a kiss," he added. "Take me back to that field of sheep-droppings."

She laughed loudly. "And who said romance was dead?" Mark looked across at his father, just entering the room, on the arm of Becky Masters.

"From son to father, eh?" said Natasha. "She really is unbelievable."

"I think it's just the star of the show out with the writer of the show," replied Mark. "I'm sure there's nothing more to it."

"How would you feel if there *were* something to it?" she asked.

"I couldn't care less," replied Mark. "My father has gone through a string of women. I no longer care what he does."

"I didn't mean about *him*," she said.

He stared at her, eyes wide. "Oh, I see! You mean how would I feel about Becky?"

"Yes."

"I can't even be bothered to answer that," he replied, adding, "go on ... give us a kiss."

She laughed again.

"Well, you two look as though you're having a good time," said Mark senior as he and Becky approached the table.

Natasha thought, Please don't sit here.

"May we join you?" asked Mark's father.

"Of course," replied Natasha and Mark together. They sat.

"Were you in tonight, Dad?" asked Mark.

"Yes. Good show," he said. "I think Bill's got a few comments about the second scene in the second act … but on the whole, it's still looking pretty good."

"Oh?" said Mark. "What's wrong with that scene? I thought it was one of my best."

"Actually, darling," piped up Becky, "they're *my* comments. I don't think you're playing it quite as it should be played."

Mark was annoyed. "Really?"

"I've thought so all along," she said, "but I've let you settle into the part first, before I made any suggestions."

"I like it the way it is!" snapped Mark. "I can't see that it can be any better."

"Oh, it can, Mark," said Becky. "Believe me. I think we ought to have a few rehearsals when we hit Bournemouth. Just you and me. I'm sure the scene can be really improved."

Natasha reached under the table for Mark's hand. He gave *her* hand a gentle but reassuring squeeze.

Bill Grant approached the table. "Evening all," he said. "A good show tonight, Mark," he added. "Got a few notes for you though. We'll talk about it tomorrow."

"So I've heard," grumbled Mark.

Bill turned his attention to Becky. "They want you to draw the raffle in fifteen minutes, darling," he said. "Can I introduce you to the MC?"

Becky stood. "Take me to him."

Mark senior leaned across the table and whispered to Natasha. "Will you be all right on your own for a few minutes? I want a word with Mark."

"Yes," she said, sounding curious. "Yes, I'll be okay."

Mark led his son across the ballroom towards the corridor leading to the toilets.

"What's up?" asked Mark, as soon as they were out of earshot of any of the other guests. "Is it Becky?"

"Becky?" asked his father, surprised.

"I thought you were going to tell me that you and she have got it together."

He smiled. "That's got nothing to do with what I've got to tell you, son," he said.

"But it's true?"

"Well, you know how it is, son. She's extremely attractive."

"And you're in a position of power," he replied, flatly.

"I don't want to talk about Becky Masters," went on his father. "This is far more important."

"Oh?"

"Might come as a bit of a let down, I'm afraid."

He knew immediately. "You're replacing me."

"Yes." He looked suitably saddened. "I'm sorry."

"But why?"

"We've been inundated from artists' agents since the press splashed Ashley Gibson's story right across the front pages. We've been offered the most extraordinary stars for nothing prices … stars you wouldn't have dreamed it was possible to get five years ago."

"I see."

"It makes commercial sense, boy," he tried to explain. "You're so talented, but…"

"Unknown."

"Yes."

"So who are you going for?"

"Brett Allen."

Mark was shocked. "Well, well, well!"

"Big, eh?"

"You're not kidding. That'll bring the punters in."

"So you do understand, son?"

Mark grinned. "Ah, but can he sing?"

Mark senior grinned back. "Does it matter?"

"Does Becky know?" he asked.

"Nobody knows yet," he replied. "Only Sam Coy and I know. We haven't even told Bill yet. Not until Brett Allen's signed his name on the dotted line."

"I won't say a word," Mark promised him.

"Good lad," he said. "Not even to Natasha, please."

"So, when's he joining us?"

"That's another problem," continued Mark senior. "After Bournemouth, we're pulling the show off the road. The Birmingham and Aberdeen advanced bookings weren't as healthy as they might have been anyway. And then it's back to London for a three week revamp ... and straight into the Vaudeville."

"I hope I'm not still going to be expected to understudy?" asked Mark. "Not now I've had all this acclaim."

His father put a comforting arm around his shoulder. "You're contracted for the run of the play, Mark."

Mark looked up and saw the twinkle in his father's eyes. "But no. Of course not. Not if you don't want to." He laughed. "You see how useful nepotism can be?"

Mark wondered how Natasha would react to all this. She'd be expected to stay in the production and continue as an ASM … for as long as the show ran.

"I suppose Natasha's contract is watertight?" he asked.

"Oh, I couldn't let her go, Mark," said his father. "She's far too useful. She's really talented. We need her to understudy Becky Masters. We couldn't get anyone better."

"So next week will be our last week together," he said, almost to himself. "Bournemouth."

"Yes, but don't let her know that," urged his father. "Not yet. The whole company will find out soon enough."

Mark returned to the table in a daze.

"What's up?" asked Natasha. "You look as white as a ghost."

"Must have been those sheep." He tried to laugh. "Perhaps I'm allergic to them."

"Mark!" she scolded him. "What's wrong?"

"Nothing's wrong!" he assured her. "Nothing at all."

15

Roger had seemed sad to see them leave, hugging Natasha before helping her down the path with her heavy suitcase.

"*He* might've already climbed that golden ladder to the sun," he'd whispered, referring to Mark, who was following on behind, "but you keep it up, Angel Face, and you'll soon find yourself eclipsing him."

Natasha helped Cyndy to wrap the photo frames and candlesticks carefully in sheets of newspaper before laying them in the removal crates, supervised from time to time by the stage manager who was organizing the complicated business of a "get-out".

"It's like moving house," moaned Natasha. "I'm dripping with sweat." She mopped her brow and then looked at her watch. It was one o'clock in the morning and there was still so much to do.

"You'll get used to it when you've done it as many times as I have," giggled Cyndy, who energetically raced around gathering up the props and more bundles of old newspapers. "I love get-outs. They're full of such … expectations; moving on and all that. You never know what you're going to face when you reach the next town. It's great."

"I'd rather've travelled with the actors," argued Natasha. "They've got the same expectations without all this back-breaking work."

Cyndy laughed. "That's because you aspire to becoming an actress. It's different for me. I can't wait to be a stage manager." She sighed. "I remember when we were in Billingham, doing *A Christmas Carol*…"

Natasha's mind began to wander, cutting out Cyndy's relentless chuntering. She wondered if Mark would have arrived in Bournemouth by now. He'd decided to travel immediately the curtain had fallen on Brighton's last performance, taking an offer of a lift from Jason, whose rust-dotted Mini they'd earlier packed to bursting with pieces of luggage.

Had Natasha been train-travelling with the rest of the cast on Sunday morning, Mark would have gone with them … naturally. But as she and Cyndy were travelling overnight in the get-out lorry, he'd leapt at the chance of a gratis journey with his red-headed understudy.

"Is he staying in the same digs as us?" asked Cyndy, suddenly, sensing that Natasha's mind was elsewhere.

"Who?"

She laughed. "Mark, of course."

Natasha was surprised at the comment. "The

same digs as *us*?" she gasped. "Why? Where are you staying?"

"Melton Court," replied Cyndy.

Natasha fought desperately to hide her disappointment. It hadn't occurred to her that she might not be alone with Mark, as she was in Brighton.

"Didn't you know?" asked Cyndy.

"No." Natasha began to pack the scatter-cushions on top of the wrapped candlesticks.

"It'll be a laugh," went on Cyndy. "You, me and Mark in the same digs. It'll be fun."

Jason and Mark took a long breakfast in a motorway cafe, aware that their respective landlords wouldn't welcome their arrival before seven a.m.

"Do you want more coffee?" asked Jason.

Mark yawned. "I think I'd better. I need something to keep me awake. This wasn't a very good idea, was it?"

Jason agreed. "We should have waited till the morning to travel."

"It'll be a wasted day," grumbled Mark. "I'll have to go to bed as soon as we book into the digs."

"You could always sleep on the beach," suggested Jason. "It looks like it's going to be a scorcher today."

Mark laughed. "You only want me to get sunstroke, so's you can take over the part."

Jason gulped, nervously. "Oh, don't say that," he said. "I'm not ready for it. I don't even know all the lines yet. If I had to go on, I'd die."

"Don't worry," Mark grinned at him. "I'm quite healthy. You won't be going on this week."

"Maybe by the time we get to Aberdeen," continued Jason. "I would have had a few rehearsals by then."

Mark said nothing. The cast would soon be told that the show was pulling off the road after Bournemouth; neither Jason nor the rest of the cast would ever get to Aberdeen.

"So where are you staying?" asked Jason.

Mark took out a crumpled piece of paper from his pocket and read. "Melton Court."

"Oh," said Jason, sounding disappointed. "I'm at Friary Road, near the fire-station … wherever that is." He took out his road plan of Bournemouth, issued to all the cast … and began to study it.

A thin, elderly, pinched-nosed woman in a dressing-gown opened the door to the Melton Court address.

"Mark *who*?" she asked.

"Fallon. I'm with the tour of *A Stranger Love*."

"Oh, yes," she said. "I did have you down as coming, but they changed it."

"*Who* changed it?" asked Mark.

"I don't know," replied the woman. She looked at her watch. It was seven-thirty. She tutted. "I was only just up. I haven't got any breakfasts to do this morning. It *is* Sunday, you know," she added accusingly.

"I'm sorry," said Mark, "but this is the address I was given."

"I've got two girls coming," she told him. "I *did* have you, but they swapped it for a girl. I had a call yesterday afternoon."

"But …"

"I'm sorry," said the woman, "but you'll have to sort it out with your producer, or whoever. I've only got two rooms and they're booked for two girls." She shut the door.

Mark ambled down the path towards the Mini, as Jason leaned out of his rolled-down window. "Problems?"

"You could say that," he sighed "I've got nowhere to stay."

The stage manager approached Natasha as she was rolling up the goatskin rug and attempting to tie it with string.

"I take it you need to go back to your digs before we set off?" he said.

"No," she replied. "I've checked out. I've put my suitcase in the prop room."

"Damn!" he cursed.

"What's up?"

"I wanted you to give a message to Mark. What time do you think he'll get up?"

"He's gone," she informed him. "He left straight after the show. Jason took him in his Mini."

"Oh, that's just great!" he snapped. "I wish he'd let me know."

"I can give him the message as soon as we arrive in Bournemouth," said Natasha. "We're in the same digs."

"That's just the problem," he sighed. "You're not! So you can't!"

Natasha was shocked. "What?"

"The management suggested I put Cyndy into the digs and move Mark to the Grand."

"But why would they want to move him?" gasped Natasha.

The stage manager shrugged. "Don't ask me. Probably so he's on easy call to do his P.A.s, I suppose. He and Becky have got radio broadcasts and things lined up for next week."

"Becky?" she half whispered.

He grinned. "Sam Coy's picking up the tab so Mark should be delighted. It'll save him a few quid."

"And Becky's at the Grand too, is she?"

"Yes. And Mark Leighson, I believe." He lowered his voice and told Natasha, confidently, "I think they're having a thing together."

Natasha gripped the goatskin until her knuckles turned white. "Who?" Her voice was trembling.

"Mark and Becky."

Natasha paled.

Cyndy, overhearing, approached. "I think he means Becky and Mark *senior*, Natasha," she said, kindly, noting the panic set on Natasha's face. "Mark's father."

"So, what are we going to do?" Cyndy asked. "It puts me in a bit of difficulty, doesn't it? Am I staying at Melton Court, or aren't I?"

"Don't worry," replied the stage manager. "I just hope Jason's not switched off his mobile."

Jason *hadn't* switched off his mobile.

"That'll be my partner," he sheepishly grinned at Mark. He pulled the car into the kerb and reached behind him, picking up the phone from the rear seat. "It'll be to find out if I've arrived safely."

Mark was surprised when he heard Jason say, "Oh, sure. Just a minute. He's here." He handed the phone across. "It's for you, Mark."

It was the last thing that Mark had expected ... or wanted. He unpacked his bag in the hotel room and lay on his bed to doze. It was certainly a luxurious place to stay, but without Natasha it meant nothing to him. He wondered what she'd say when she arrived at the digs, to find he was staying on the other side of the town. And he wondered how she'd react when she discovered that Becky Masters had been booked into the same hotel.

He woke at lunch time, hurriedly showered and set off for Melton Court, hoping that Natasha would have arrived.

"We don't have visitors just popping in!" said the pinched-nosed woman. "And anyway, they've only just got here. They're unpacking."

"Could you let her know I'm down the road at McDonalds?" asked Mark. "I'll wait for her there."

"I'll tell her," she said, huffily, before slamming the door in his face.

"You don't mind me here, do you?" asked Cyndy as she flopped on to a seat beside Mark.

Natasha sat opposite them, looking despairingly at him.

"Only I'm starving," went on Cyndy. "What do you want, Natasha? I'll get it."

"Just a coffee, please," replied Natasha.

"You sure? Nothing to eat?"

"No, thanks."

"What about you, Mark?"

"No, I'm all right, thanks, Cyndy," he said.

Cyndy crossed to the counter.

"Sorry," sighed Natasha. "She just tagged along. It would've been too cruel to tell her I didn't want her to come."

Mark reached across the table and took her hand. "You look tired."

"I am," she replied. "It's been a killer of a job. I hate it." She sighed deeply. "I wish I was acting. I'll never ASM again."

"Cyndy seems okay about it," he said.

"She loves it," explained Natasha. "She's even volunteered to do the get-in on her own tomorrow morning."

"Let her," said Mark with a grin. "We can go for another picnic."

Natasha laughed.

"I'm sorry about the digs arrangement," said Mark. "I didn't get any say in it. They've booked me into the Grand Hotel."

"I know," replied Natasha. "With Becky."

"Yes." He grimaced.

"And your father."

He was stunned. "My father?"

"Apparently."

"He didn't say he was coming on to Bournemouth."

She was embarrassed. Maybe it wasn't true. Perhaps the stage manager had got it wrong.

"I only hope we've got some time together," she

said. "Haven't you got some personal appearances to do this week? Radio interviews and things?"

"You seem to know more about it than I do," he replied. "I hope they haven't got too much lined up for me. Not in this weather. I thought we could spend our days together on the beach."

She shrugged. "I've got some rehearsal days with Jason, as well," she said. "So … what with your P.A.s and my rehearsals … and separate digs, it looks as though we won't be seeing much of each other this week."

He let go of her hand and stared down into his empty polystyrene coffee cup. "No. It looks like it," he said sadly.

She tried to cheer him. "Don't worry," she said. "We'll make up for it in Birmingham and Aberdeen."

He desperately wanted to tell her. But he'd promised not to say a word. Bournemouth was to be their last week together. Then he was leaving the show. They had to grab some time together. Had to! Soon she'd be told, along with the rest of the company, that Bournemouth was the end of the road … and he wondered how she'd react.

"What the hell are you doing, Dad?" asked Mark as soon as Becky had left the hotel dining-room to powder her nose.

He grinned. "What do you mean?"

"It's me she was after, you know."

"So? And now it's me." He suddenly looked serious. "You're not jealous, are you, son?"

"No!" Mark exploded. "Of course not!"

His father looked around the room at the other

diners. "Hush. We don't want them all to know our family affairs!" He laughed at his choice of words.

"As long as you're sure she's not using you."

"Using me? How could she be using me? She's already got the job."

"Not the London contract," he said.

"She has now," Mark's father informed him.

Mark sat back in his chair and sighed deeply. "I see."

"Oh, come on, Mark!" his father snapped. "She's perfect for it. Sam Coy and I agreed ages ago that she should go into London. We never really had any doubts about her. It was Ashley we were in two minds about. So ... if she knows her job is safe, she can't be using me, can she."

"Unless..."

"Unless what?"

"Unless..." He hardly dared say it. "Unless it's to get to me."

Mark senior laughed. "Didn't you once tell her that she was only spending time with you, to get to me?"

Mark blushed. "She didn't *tell* you that?"

"She did."

"How embarrassing."

"That's life, son!" grinned Mark senior. "Don't worry about it."

"So, what else has she told you about me?"

"Nothing. Except you seem to be infatuated by her understudy. Well ... that's how *she* put it." He laughed.

"I'm in love with Natasha, Dad," he said, firmly.

"Love?" replied his father, cynically. "What's love?"

Becky returned and sat. "I've ordered a bottle of champagne," she said. "It's on its way."

"Oh, really?" smiled Mark senior. "Celebrating something, are we?"

"How about my first starring role in London? With the hunky Brett Allen."

Mark gasped. "You *know* about Brett Allen?" He turned to his father. "She *knows*?"

"Well, I thought it was only fair that I told her, Mark," said his father, guiltily.

"Of course I know!" said Becky. "I've known for ages."

"How do you mean, ages?" Mark's voice was rising, angrily.

His father tried to calm him. "I told Becky just after I'd told you."

Becky looked surprised but a quick glare from Mark senior warned her to say no more.

"But *I* wasn't allowed to tell *Natasha*."

"I *am* the star of this show, Mark!" said Becky.

Mark senior reached out and grabbed Mark's arm. "*Everyone* will know tomorrow, son," he said, softly. "The call has been made for an hour earlier than usual. And that's why. Sam's coming down to Bournemouth. And we're going to inform the whole company before the show."

Mark stood. "I'm going to bed!"

"But the champagne hasn't arrived yet," said Becky.

"I don't want any," replied Mark.

"Don't forget to put in your alarm call at the

desk," his father reminded him. "You've got a press call at nine with the *Hampshire and Dorset Times*."

Mark flashed a look at Becky. "I'm busy tomorrow morning," he said. "Let the star do it. I'm going out with the ASM."

16

"You again?" said the unsmiling, pinched-nosed woman. She looked at her watch. "It's a bit early, isn't it? I don't even think she's up yet."

"Mark?" a voice called from the end of the hall. Natasha approached. "Hi!" she said, sounding surprised. "What are you doing here at this hour?"

The sour-faced landlady gave both of them a hard look before retreating to her breakfast room, leaving them to talk on the doorstep.

"It's not that early," he replied. "It's nine o'clock. Feels more like twelve though, it's so hot."

"You'll have to give me ten minutes," Natasha grinned excitedly.

He beamed. "So you are free, then?"

"I did as you said," she giggled. "I let Cyndy do the get-in. She seemed really keen, so..."

"Great!" he said. "I'll go and get us a picnic and I'll meet you back here."

She laughed.

"And don't forget your swimming things," he added. "You'll *need* them."

The harbour was full of mini-craft; small yachts and dinghies which, outlined against the cloudless, bright blue sky, made Bournemouth suddenly appear like a Mediterranean port.

As they waited for the ferry to arrive, Natasha dashed into a nearby shop and returned with a white baseball cap which she placed on her blonde head.

"Does it look awful?" she asked.

Mark laughed. "It's not very elegant."

"It's the cheapest one they had," she smiled. "The top of my head felt as though it was on fire."

"I know what you mean," said Mark. "I wish I'd brought some shorts with me. My jeans are soaking with sweat."

"It'll be cooler over on Shell Bell," a voice informed them.

Natasha turned to face a tiny man with white hair atop a mahogany skin. He was in his seventies; his face ravaged – more by sunshine than by age.

"There's a cool breeze over there," he added. "If that's where you're going, of course."

"They told me at my hotel that it's all golden sands and dunes. Is that right?" asked Mark.

"It's like nowhere on Earth," replied the man. "You can keep your Majorcas and all those. Bournemouth knocks them into a cocked hat."

Mark suspected that the man had never been anywhere else *but* Bournemouth.

"Lived here all my life," he went on. "And since I retired I've done this trip every day, come rain or shine."

"Really?" said Natasha, trying to sound interested, but wishing he'd leave her and Mark on their own. She hoped he had no intention of sitting near them on the beach.

"Yes," he continued. "Down here to Sandbanks … across to Shell Bay on the ferry … a long walk up the beach … and back home for tea."

"It can't be very nice in the winter," grimaced Mark.

"No. But at least there's no snakes," the old man replied with a toothless grin. "Not like there are in the summer."

Natasha felt her body tense up at the suggestion of snakes.

"What sort of snakes?" asked Mark, curiously.

"All sorts." He laughed until he coughed. "Part of it over there's a nature reserve," he said, "so you get all sorts of funny things crawling around."

Natasha grabbed Mark's arm. "I don't think I want to go," she said.

Mark squeezed her hand, reassuringly. "Ferry's arrived," he said. "Come on."

The ferry took just two minutes to cross the bay, and as all the foot-passengers scrambled off, allowing the few cars that had been carried to disembark behind them, a refreshing breeze engulfed the overheated holiday makers.

"Ooh, that's nice," sighed Natasha.

"Told you," said the old man who'd kept close

beside them as they were ferried across.

Natasha and Mark removed their trainers and socks at the water's edge. Mark rolled up his 501s to just below the knees and pulled off his tee-shirt, which he pushed into the carrier bag holding their picnic.

They'd both hoped that the old man would walk ahead, leaving them in peace, but he waited until they were ready to stroll along the long golden beach. Mark walked with his feet in the water, holding Natasha's hand as she strolled beside him, indenting the damp sand with her bare toes.

"It's really beautiful," said Mark. "It's like one of those uncrowded beaches in northern Spain."

"You can keep Spain," grumbled the man, who was slowly walking just ahead of them. "There's nothing like Bournemouth."

Mark and Natasha looked at each other and grinned.

"Here we go again," she mouthed to Mark.

"Of course … you don't get *snakes* in Spain," lectured the old man, incorrectly.

Mark asked him, "They're just grass snakes, I take it?"

He turned his head as he continued to walk, "No," he replied. "Not just grass snakes. There's adders here too. Hundreds of them."

Natasha's grip on Mark's hand tightened.

"So when you go up into the sand dunes … and you'll be bound to do that, you being young lovers and all that – " he grinned – " just you be careful. Don't tread daintily, like. You have to stamp. That way, the adders know you're there and they slither away. They don't like you, any more than you like them."

"Suppose they bit you?" asked Natasha, fearfully. "Would you die?"

"Might do," replied the man, matter-of-factly. "They've been known to kill little kiddies and dogs with one bite."

"But not fully grown adults?" asked Mark.

"Might do," the man said. "Certainly give you a nasty lick." He laughed heartily, cackled a little, then coughed.

"Come on!" Mark yelled suddenly as he began to drag Natasha up the beach towards the dunes.

She squealed. "No! Mark!"

"You go!" the man called after them. "Find yourself one of those lovey-dovey dunes. But watch out for snakes."

Natasha was horrified as Mark led her along the tiny sandy paths, overgrown with bracken and purple headed gorse, stamping all the while in order to scare off possible lurking adders. Away from the sea, the acoustics changed completely. No sound of waves lapping on to the shore … no sound of children laughing, nor sunbathers' idle chat. Just the low hum of bees, droning monotonously as they hovered and hopped from plant to shrub.

"How about here?" Mark asked the terrified Natasha. He pointed to a hollow between two dunes, just big enough to fit two bodies and a carrier bag.

"Is it safe, do you think?"

"Of course it's safe," he grinned. "Let's leave the

bees and the snakes to get on with their business." He smiled impishly at her. "And we can get on with ours."

As they stepped into the hollow, a lizard, cleverly camouflaged against a small stone, scurried away.

Mark looked at Natasha, expecting her to scream and rush back to the beach. She gave no reaction at all. Mark realized that she hadn't seen it, and decided not to mention it. He peeled off his jeans and stood handsomely in his swimming trunks, staring at her, as she settled into the hollow in her bright yellow bikini.

"Bees'll love that," he grinned. "You look like a buttercup."

She reached up for his hand and pulled him down beside her.

"Picnic? A little doze? Or a cuddle?" he asked with a smile. "What shall we have first?"

She laughed. "A doze and a cuddle!" she said. "At the same time. Then a swim … then the picnic. Okay?"

"Okay," he agreed.

They lay face to face, arms wrapped around each other … and both of them pretended to sleep.

"I'd like to speak to Becky Masters," said the voice on the other end of the line. "I think she's in room twenty-six."

The hotel's desk clerk asked him to wait while he tried her number.

"I'm sorry, sir," he said finally. "There's no reply."

"Can I leave a message?" he asked.

"Of course, sir." He picked up a pencil and was poised to write.

"Tell her that Damien rang and that I'm coming to Bournemouth tonight and I've booked to see the show again. I'll pick her up at the hotel about five o'clock."

"Thank you, sir."

"Have you got that?" he asked.

"Yes, sir. I'll leave the note for room twenty-six."

Natasha opened her eyes and examined the face before her. How could she ever have thought that he was plain looking? Just an ordinary boy-next-door? He couldn't have grown more handsome over the past few weeks. He must always have looked like this. And yet, during their first few days together, she hadn't noticed the perfectly shaped, though tiny, button nose; the thick, dark eyebrows ... and the sensuously dimpled chin which she longed to touch. She couldn't lift her arms, which were entwined with his, without disturbing him, so she tenderly placed her lips on to his dimple and kissed it. She could feel his heartbeat next to her, suddenly quickening. She placed her lips close to one of his eyelids and gently blew. And she saw the eyelids slightly flicker into a smile. She lowered her mouth and place it on his, not kissing him, just brushing her lips against his. She heard him moan gently with pleasure as he responded to her closeness. He opened his eyes just briefly to see her beautiful face so near to him. Then he closed them again, sighed deeply and lifted his hand, running his fingertips through her hair as he kissed her with uncontrollable passion.

He suddenly stopped and scrambled to his feet. "Race you to the sea!" he said.

She stood. "We can't just leave our clothes here."

"Who'd want a tatty pair of Levis and a sweat soaked tee-shirt?" he laughed.

"What about my new hat?" she giggled.

He picked up the baseball cap and plonked it on her head. "Wear it!" he said. He grabbed her hand and led her, running and thudding through the gorse, scattering the bees and causing any would-be-deadly serpents to slink away in fear of their lives.

They hurtled across the sandy beach and down towards the sea, where they ran straight in, gasping as the chill water rose above their waists.

Natasha screamed. "It's freezing."

"Don't be such a wet," he said. He placed his hands on her shoulders and pushed her down, until her head ducked under the water. She came up spluttering and giggling.

"My hat! It's ruined."

He put his arms around her and pulled her to him. She thrilled at his wet body touching hers. They held each other tightly and kissed, totally oblivious to the other paddlers, swimmers and tiny sandcastle-builders.

He suddenly pulled away from her and ducked beneath the water, disappearing in the sand-churned murk. She feared what he was up to. She felt him brush one leg and she shrieked loudly … the shriek quickly turning to a giggle as she then felt him dive between her legs and slowly rise out of the water, lifting her high upon his shoulders.

"I'm the King of the Castle!" she yelled, remembering her yesteryear playground chant. "I'm the King of the Castle!" she repeated. She looked down at him and grinned, ruffling his wet hair with her fingers. "And you're the dirty rascal!"

He gently lowered her back to her feet. "I'm not, you know," he said, sounding almost serious.

She rubbed his cheek with the palm of her hand.

"Picnic time?" he asked, brightly.

"Picnic time!" she agreed.

They began to stroll back to the shore.

"I don't know how I'll cope," she said. "A picnic without sheep-droppings."

"Aah, but plenty of snake droppings," he reminded her gleefully, adding, "Do you think snakes like cheese and tomato sandwiches?"

"Take a bite," she said as she stood holding a large green apple towards him.

"Leading me astray, eh?" he asked, his eyes twinkling. He leapt to his feet. "Tempting me with forbidden fruit?"

"Do you *need* tempting?" Natasha replied with a gentle giggle. She looked at the apple, curiously. "Anyway, who says it's forbidden?"

He took the apple from her and bit into it. Then he handed it to her. "Your turn."

"No thanks," she grinned. "I don't want any."

He shivered suddenly. "Wind's blowing up. We'd better get dressed."

"And time we got back to town," she added. "We

don't want to be late for the show, do we?"

"Don't we? I could stay here for ever." He pulled on his tee-shirt and flopped back into the dune, reaching up for her hand.

"Sit down, Natasha," he said. "I've got something to tell you."

She sensed there was something seriously wrong.

She sat.

"I wondered where you'd got to," Mark senior said, irritably. He strode across the yucca-filled lobby of Radio Bourne towards the reception desk, where Becky Masters had just announced her arrival. "I've been waiting outside Sainsbury's as we planned."

Becky greeted him with a kiss on the cheek. "They wanted photos as well," she explained, "so it took longer than I thought. I dashed back to the hotel for some decent clothes for the shoot, but you'd already left. I left a note for you with the desk clerk in case you came back."

"I didn't go back," he told her.

"Obviously not," she grinned. "Or you wouldn't have been standing outside Sainsbury's in the blazing sun, would you?"

Mark senior looked at his watch. "What time are you on the air?"

"About four, so the researcher said. They hoped that your Mark'd be here too."

"Fat chance," he replied. "He wasn't too happy last night, was he?"

"Strange lad you've got," she mused.

The researcher arrived and shook her hand. "Miss Masters?"

"That's me," she smiled. "And this is the writer of the novel, *A Stranger Love*," she added. "Maryanne ... a.k.a. Mark ... Leighson."

They strolled slowly back towards the ferry, Natasha feeling numb from the news she'd received.

"And you couldn't be persuaded to stay?" she asked.

He shrugged. "Would you?"

"No," she replied sadly. "I suppose not."

"If I return to understudying I could be at it for years, Natasha. I've got to grab this opportunity. My agent could put me up for leading roles at the moment. I mean ... the reviews have been great."

"I know," she sighed resignedly.

He put his arms around her. "I'm sorry."

Tears filled her eyes. "Don't be. It's not your fault. That's life ... I suppose."

"Even if I go away on tour, I'll phone you at the theatre every day," he promised.

"Yes." A tear rolled down her cheek and she quickly brushed it away.

"And if I don't get a job, I shall be hanging around the stage door every night, waiting for you."

"You will get a job," she said, positively. "You're very talented, Mark."

"Thanks." He hugged her tightly.

"I just hope that when you fly off to Hollywood to make your first movie, you won't forget me ...

setting candlesticks and photo frames all in the wrong places." She tried to laugh. It didn't come easy.

He walked on, his arm still wrapped around her, in silence.

"So this is the last week," she said. "It'll be quite a bombshell for all the cast tonight, won't it?"

"You could say that. Especially for Jason. I think he'd cope being an understudy to me. But to understudy Brett Allen...?"

"He'll be terrified," she agreed.

"I've got lots of press calls and things this week," he said, seriously. "So, you will understand if we can't spend any more days like this together, won't you?"

The reality hit her. This was her last full day with him. I can't bear it, she thought. "Of course I understand," she said.

"Is Miss Masters in?" asked Damien.

The desk clerk checked the board behind him. Her key was on the hook. "No, sir," he replied. "She's out."

"I rang this morning," Damien said, angrily. "I left a message for her."

"I wasn't on duty this morning, sir," replied the clerk. "But I'll just check."

He found two notes for room twenty-six.

"It's here, sir," he said. "I'm sorry. She hasn't picked it up. But she may have left a note for you. Is your name Mark?"

He was curious. And very suspicious.

"Yes," he said.

"Here, sir." The clerk handed him two notes; one addressed to Ms Masters. The other simply said, "Mark."

17

Natasha announced on the tannoy, "Beginners for Act One please, ladies and gentlemen. Miss Masters and Mr Fallon, your calls, please. Your calls, please, Miss Masters and Mr Fallon. Thank you."

Mark kissed her on the cheek and laughed. "Why call me? I'm here, already."

She smiled up at him from her prompt-corner seat and shrugged. "I don't know. Tradition?"

He looked so handsome in his costume and she found it almost too difficult to believe that, just a few hours before, they were entwined in a sand dune, whispering sweet nothings.

Becky arrived in the corner. "Ready?" she asked Mark, flatly.

She walked on to the set and positioned herself on the chaise-longue. Mark looked at Natasha, gave a flicker of a smile and joined Becky on the set.

"Nice day?" asked Becky, hardly looking at him.

"Yes, thanks. You?"

"All day on the sands, I suppose?"

"That's right."

"You should've been at the radio station with me!" she said, harshly. "You're so unprofessional, Mark."

"Oh, thanks!" he replied.

"You've got so much to learn in this business," she added.

"Look – " he said, angrily – "I'm being sacked at the end of this week, so why should I go out promoting the show, for someone else?"

"Firstly, you're not being sacked!" she argued. "You can return to your job of understudying, if you want to. If you choose to leave, that's up to you."

He shrugged.

"And secondly," she went on, "I'm sure your father would appreciate your help on this one."

"I'm going to do all the rest of the promos this week!" he said. "But today was my last day with Natasha. I'm sorry, Becky. But that's important to me."

"More important than your career?"

"Yes. In fact!"

She sneered. "Then why are you leaving the show ... *and her*?"

He had no answer. She was right.

They heard Natasha give her stage management instruction, firstly to the lighting box, "House lights down." There was a pause. "Curtain up."

Becky looked into Mark's eyes.

The curtain rose.

Becky delivered her first line, "So how long will you be away?"

Mark glowered at her. "Look, Sarah, don't let's start all this again."

Damien had arrived at the stage door just after the actors' half-hour call.

"I'm sorry, sir," the stage doorkeeper informed him. "It's after the half. I can't let anyone backstage."

Damien glared at him. "Put a call through to her room!" he demanded. "She'll see me."

"Miss Masters sees no one after the half," he said. "I'm sorry."

"I'm not one of her stage door Johnnies!" snapped Damien. "I happen to be her fiancé."

"I'm sorry!" said the doorkeeper. "I'll let her know you called. Perhaps you could call back as soon as the show's down. That's at about ten-thirty."

Damien glared at the man, turned on his heels and left the theatre.

The chorus had gathered in the wings for the beginning of act two. Natasha and Cyndy cleaned and reset the ashtray, straightened the rug and moved the vase of flowers. Then Natasha returned to the prompt-corner and hushed the chorus, most of whom were unusually noisy. The earlier news about the revamp and the tour cancellation had disturbed them and many had called their London agents determined to find out if Sam Coy could do this at such short notice.

"Settle down please, Ladies and Gentlemen," said Natasha, "the curtain's about to rise."

Mark and Becky hurried from their dressing-rooms and on to the stage. They stood by the coffee table and held each other in a loving embrace, although not a whisper was passed between them.

This was the scene which Natasha hated; the tender love scene ending with the long, passionate kiss. The scene during which Natasha usually turned her back on the action and re-arranged misplaced props on the prop-table. Tonight she couldn't do that. The stage manager had, for the first time, put her in charge of the book ... and Natasha had to watch all the action ... just in case one of the actors should "dry".

Fuming about the way the stage doorkeeper had treated him, Damien had spent the first act in the stalls' bar, knocking back large whiskies. From time to time he took the note from his pocket and studied it. There was no doubt about it now. His suspicions were confirmed. It was addressed to "Mark", and it was a very affectionate billet-doux. A pathetic, childish love note, proving once and for all what he'd known all along. Becky was involved with Mark Fallon!

The more he drank, the cloudier the words became, though they were gaining, rather than losing, potency. On hearing the last bell, warning the audience that the curtain on act two was about to rise, he staggered to his seat in the back stalls and stared almost blindly through the dimming auditorium towards the rising curtain. And there he saw them, holding each other; Jonathan and Sarah ... Mark and Becky!

JONATHAN: ... I know you'll find this difficult to believe, but I've never stopped loving you. Never.

SARAH: Oh, Jonathan.

Mark kissed Becky, squeezing her tightly.

As Becky tenderly ran her fingers up his spine, Natasha looked down at the prompt copy ... not wanting to watch.

And the drunken Damien rose from his seat and yelled, "Becky! Don't!" He began to cry. "Don't! Please!" he yelled again.

Heads turned to face him and an usher rushed down the aisle towards Damien's seat.

On stage, Becky froze. She recognized the voice.

"I love you, Becky!" he called out.

Embarrassed members of the audience began to giggle, while others angrily tried to hush the heckler.

"This way, sir," said the usher, putting out his hand to take Damien's arm. "Let's get some air, shall we?"

Damien was willingly led away, deeply distressed, with a head spinning with alcohol and a heart racing with jealousy.

"What's going on?" Cyndy whispered to Natasha.

Natasha was as ignorant as Cyndy. "I've no idea. Someone's yelling out, I think."

Becky pulled away from Mark's embrace, her heart pounding, her mind struggling for the next line.

Mark knew she'd dried. He wondered how he could get her back on to the script.

"She's gone!" whispered Cyndy. "She's dried!"

Natasha began to panic. She'd momentarily lost her place in the book. "Oh, no ... oh, no."

Cyndy leaned over her shoulder and quickly ran her finger down the script, finding the kiss ... and the line which followed.

"Will you stay?!" she yelled out.

Becky heard the line. But she was rigid with stage fright. It was the first time in her career that she'd dried during a show.

"Will you stay?" called Cyndy again.

Becky could see only Damien's face in her mind ... the play was totally forgotten ... and she wondered why he'd come to Bournemouth ... and she realized that someone must have told him about her liaison with Mark Leighson. And the echo of Damien's pathetic cry had made her heart beat so fast. And she felt so guilty. How could she let him down like that? Why hadn't she told him, long, long ago?

"Will you stay?" Cyndy yelled.

"Will you stay?" Becky repeated. "Tell me you'll stay this time, Jonathan."

Natasha and Cyndy breathed a sigh of relief.

"She's back," whispered Cyndy.

Natasha reached out and affectionately squeezed

her hand. "Thanks, Cyndy."

Cyndy smiled. "Part of the job," she replied, flippantly.

As the curtain fell on the assembled cast taking their final curtain call, Becky raced into the wings, stabbing an accusing finger at Natasha.

"Where was the line?" she shrieked.

"We gave you the line," Natasha stammered, staring in amazement at the thunderous face before her. She suddenly felt very frightened.

The experienced Cyndy was much cooler. "I gave you the line, Becky. You just didn't pick it up."

Mark arrived behind them. "I heard the line, Becky," he said.

Becky's furious face suddenly changed to despair. She burst into tears, howling, "I've never been so humiliated in all my life."

Mark put his arm around her. "Come on, Becky," he said. "Let's get you to your room."

As he led the sobbing Becky away from the wings, Cyndy smiled warmly at Natasha. "You all right?"

"I'm fine," she replied. "Let's reset these props, eh?"

"Sit there," said Mark. "I'll get you a drink."

Becky slumped into the armchair in her dressing-room and dried her tears.

"How do you think he found out?" she asked.

"Don't ask me," said Mark. He looked at her in the dressing-table mirror, as he poured her a small vodka. "I hope you don't think I told him."

"Not *you*," she sniffled.

"Nor Natasha," he assured her.

"It's all so unfair," said Becky. "There's nothing between your father and me. Not really. It's only a bit of harmless fun, and both of us know it. We just enjoy each other's company, that's all."

"It obviously doesn't look that way to Damien," sighed Mark.

"No."

"You should have told Damien you wanted to end the relationship," he lectured.

"I know," she said. "Well … he knows now."

"But he won't let you go that easily," said Mark. "You heard him. He was almost begging you not to leave him."

"Yes."

He brought the vodka to her and knelt by her chair. "Here."

"Thanks." She didn't take it. She stretched out her hand and gently stroked his cheek. "I still feel the same way about you, you know," she said.

He looked away. "Don't," he replied softly.

"Oh, don't worry, Mark," she continued. "I know there's no chance. I can see you're in love with Natasha."

"Very much so," he sighed.

They were silent.

She took the vodka and sipped it. "You should stay with the show. She'll miss you if you leave."

"I've been thinking…" he began.

"And so will *I*," she added as an afterthought.

The dressing-room door suddenly burst open and Damien stared down at them.

182

"Oh, very cosy!" he slurred.

Becky leapt to her feet. "Damien!"

He glowered at Mark, tears filling his eyes. "Thank you," he said. "Thank you for destroying our relationship."

Mark gasped. "What? Damien, I haven't…"

Damien held out the note towards Mark. "This is what she wrote to you," he said.

Becky recognized the piece of paper and took it from Damien's hand, just as Mark senior rushed into the room.

"What's been going on?" he asked. "I miss one show, and the stage manager tells me all hell breaks loose."

Damien turned on him. "It was your leading actress and your dear son!" he said.

Becky went to him in an attempt to calm him. "Damien," she whispered, comfortingly. "You've got it all wrong."

The big man crumpled into her arms.

Becky looked pleadingly at father and son. "Will you leave us?" she said, softly. "Damien and I have got to talk."

18

A small bistro in the town centre was pleased to welcome the late arrivals, especially as the staff had been informed that the diners were stars of *A Stranger Love*, now playing to capacity audiences at their local theatre. The waiter was disappointed when he noted that Becky Masters wasn't among the troupe, although he treated the three unknowns with great courtesy.

"I made sure you didn't miss out this time, Natasha," said Mark senior as the waiter led them to a small table at the back of the bistro.

"Thanks," she smiled.

"So, what's this in honour of?" asked his son, good humouredly. "An apology dinner for replacing me with Brett Allen?"

"You know it's not," he said. "It's more of an apology for dragging you into this business with Becky Masters and partner."

Mark grinned. "I could've been thumped, you know."

"I know. I'm really sorry, son."

The waiter handed them the wine-list.

"Where are you going to stay tonight?" asked Natasha. "You can't go back to that hotel. Becky's taken Damien there."

"I'm going home," he informed them. "I wasn't intending to stay tonight, anyway."

"Oh?" said Mark, surprised. "You didn't say."

"It was going to be a secret," said Mark senior, "but I may as well tell you now. I've got to be at Gatwick Airport first thing in the morning."

Mark knew. "Really?" he said, excitedly. He grabbed Natasha's hand.

"What's up?" she asked, with a quizzical smile.

"It's Mum, isn't it?" grinned Mark.

"Yes," his father confirmed. "She wants to see her darling boy playing a leading role." He laughed. "So she's speeding from Spain, before it's too late."

"Great!" yelled Mark. "Fantastic." He squeezed Natasha's hand. "You'll love her!" he said.

"And I'm sure your mother will love Natasha," added Mark senior. He smiled wistfully as he whispered across the table to Natasha, "You remind me of her, when she was young. You're very much alike."

Mark wasn't so sure. "Really?"

"Oh, very much," said his father.

"Is Manolo coming with her?" he asked.

"No. He's too busy. But he sends his love."

Mark turned to Natasha. "He's great. When we go to Spain together, he'll make sure we have a good time."

Natasha's heart skipped.

"So, you're going to Spain together, are you?" asked Mark Senior. "*When*, may I ask? Don't forget Natasha's tied up with this show for the foreseeable future."

"And *Natasha* and *I* are tied up together for the foreseeable future," grinned Mark. He kissed Natasha on the cheek. "So this year … next year … whenever. But I'm determined to take her to the villa."

"I take it you don't want to see your mother before the show?" asked Mark senior.

"Definitely not!" laughed his son. "And I don't want to know where she's sitting. I'll be a bundle of nerves as it is, knowing she's out front."

The wine-waiter returned to take the order.

"Shall we have some champagne?" Mark senior asked his guests.

"Why not?" replied Mark. "If Mum's on her way, we've really got something to celebrate!"

Mark took Natasha back to his hotel for a nightcap, sure that being so late, Becky and Damien would have said their goodbyes and retired for the night.

He was wrong.

Becky sat in the bar, alone, staring down into an untouched glass of vodka and tonic.

Natasha whispered before they entered, "Mark, let's go, shall we? She won't want us here."

"Look at her," said Mark sympathetically. "We can't ignore her. She looks so miserable."

He ordered two glasses of wine from the sleepy

barman and then crossed to Becky's table. Natasha followed him.

"Becky?"

She looked up, saw them and tried to smile.

"Are you all right?" Mark asked her.

She nodded. "Sit down," she croaked. Her voice was tired. Her eyes were red.

"Has he gone?" asked Mark.

"I've booked him into a room here," she replied. "He couldn't drive back tonight. He was in a bit of a state."

"He *was* very drunk," Mark agreed.

"I don't mean that," she whispered, hoarsely. She cleared her throat. "He seems quite sober now. But he's emotionally drained."

"I'm not surprised," sighed Mark.

"And I am too," she added.

"So, have you ended the relationship?" asked Mark.

She shook her head, sadly. "No. Not really. I couldn't. He was just so distraught..."

"Oh, dear!" said Mark.

Becky reached out to take his hand but, aware of Natasha's presence, she stopped herself. "It'll be all right," she unconvincingly tried to assure him, though *she* was begging assurance from *him*.

Natasha put her hand on top of Becky's. "It'll be all right, Becky," she said.

Becky smiled at her for the first time since they'd met. "Thanks Natasha." She cleared her throat again. "I'm so tired," she said. "I must get to bed or my voice will be like sandpaper tomorrow."

"It's stress," Natasha said, warmly. "You need a good night's rest."

"And we've got that local TV interview at nine," said Mark.

Becky groaned huskily. "*What* time?"

He shrugged. "Nine."

She looked at her watch.

"I'll meet you in the lobby at eight," he said. "They're sending a car for us."

Becky stood, wearily. "Make it eight-thirty, eh?"

"Okay."

She kissed Mark on the cheek. "Night, Mark."

She then kissed Natasha on the cheek.

"Night, Natasha. Thanks," she said. "And I'm sorry."

She ambled out of the hotel bar.

"Well, well, well," whispered Natasha. "She loves me ... she loves me not..."

"We'd better finish this wine, and then I'll walk you home," he said.

"I'll get a cab," she insisted. "It's late, Mark. And you've got to get your beauty sleep if you're appearing on the telly tomorrow."

"I don't need beauty sleep," he joked. "I'm beautiful enough."

She looked at him through love-clouded eyes. "Yes," she agreed. "You are."

He laughed and stood, lifting her from her bar stool and wrapping his arms around her.

"I wish I could watch you on the box tomorrow," she gently sighed, "but I've got an understudy rehearsal with Jason."

"I know you have." He gently ruffled her hair.

"Why do you want to watch me on the television, anyway?"

She shrugged. "To see that beautiful face?"

"You can see it *now*," he grinned. "And you can touch it, if you want."

She ran her fingertips across his dimpled chin and up across his smooth, smiling lips.

"You can even kiss it," he said, seductively.

She placed her lips on his and kissed.

At first he was playfully unresponsive, allowing her to take the initiative. But he could only hold out for seconds. And then he kissed her. And her fingertips began to tingle as her heart beat faster and faster. And her whole body began to tremble as her weakening legs began to feel like jelly.

He drew away from her, and whispered. "There. You couldn't feel *that* through a TV screen. That was the real thing."

Mark paced the hotel lobby, constantly eyeing his watch. Where was she? He crossed to the desk-clerk, who was occupied, sorting out the morning newspapers.

"Could you put a call through to Miss Masters' room?" he asked.

"Sorry, Mr Fallon," he replied. "I didn't see you there. She's left a note for you."

Mark read the note.

"Mark … sorry … had to go out. Make your own way to the studio. I'll see you there."

Had to go out? he thought. He assumed that it had something to do with Damien.

* * *

The PA approached Mark in the studio reception area, peering over his shoulder for Becky Masters.

"Hasn't she arrived yet?" Mark asked him.

"No. I thought she was coming with you."

Mark sighed. "I'm sorry. I don't know where she is."

The female researcher hurried from studio four. "Mark Fallon?"

"Yes."

"There's a problem," the PA informed her. "No Becky Masters."

The researcher gasped. "Where is she? We're on air in ten minutes."

"I don't know," replied Mark, agitated. "She said she'd meet me here."

"But ... our whole interview is..."

"I know," interrupted Mark. "Of course it's based around Becky's TV career." He shrugged. "I don't *like* this, but the only thing I can suggest is that you pin the story on my background. My father wrote the book of *A Stranger Love*."

The researcher looked oddly at Mark and then checked her notes. "*A Stranger Love* was written by Maryanne Leighson."

"Quite!" replied Mark. "My father! Enough of a story for you?"

"I'm sorry, Natasha," said Jason, irritably. "Can we go back on that bit?" He grinned, nervously. "I can't seem to handle props, walk and speak ... all at the same time."

She laughed and put her arms around his waist.

"It's only a letter, Jason. Of course you can do it. Hold the letter out first and wave it in my direction. Then say the line. Then cross to me."

He returned to his starting position. "Right, let's try it again," he said.

Mark entered the theatre through the stalls, with the excuse he was heading backstage via the pass-door. In truth, he was curious to watch Jason struggling with the part which one day he may play. He stared up at the stage as the spotlight fell on to Natasha's golden hair. Struck by her beauty he could hardly believe that this was the girl who fell readily into his arms. Her soft voice delivered the lines with such ease and for the first time he was without doubt that Natasha Ward was a star of the future. A big, big star. *If* she got her lucky break, of course.

The stage manager turned and saw Mark, drooling over Natasha's graceful movement around the stage.

He crossed to him and whispered, "Don't linger, Mark, there's a good lad. Jason's having enough problems as it is. If he sees you standing there, he'll be even more inhibited."

"Sorry," mouthed Mark as he strolled off towards the pass-door.

As he entered backstage, he saw Becky scurrying along the corridor towards her dressing-room.

"Becky?" he called.

She stopped and turned.

"Where the hell were you?" he asked. "They

went mad at the TV studio."

Becky tried to speak, but a husky note, forced out, threw Mark into complete panic.

"I've been to the doctor," she croaked. "It's the stress I've been through," she tried to say, but only whispered. "I've no voice, Mark. I've got to rest it for a few days."

He gasped.

"I'm sorry, Mark," she added. "But I can't go on tonight."

Jason's eye caught Mark whispering to the stage manager. He stopped in mid-line and stared.

Mark looked up at him. "Sorry, Jason. I didn't mean to put you off."

Natasha wondered what was going on. Mark and the stage manager looked very worried. "What's up?" she asked.

"We're going to free you for the rest of the day, Jason," the stage manager informed him.

Jason paled. "Why?"

"Don't worry," called Mark kindly. "It's nothing to do with *you*, Jason. It's just that *I* have to rehearse with Natasha. Immediately."

Natasha felt herself sway from side to side as the adrenalin surged through her body. "Is it Becky?" she asked, fearfully.

The stage manager nodded. "She's off, Natasha. And you're on!"

Mark knocked on Becky's dressing-room door.

"Come in!" called a trembling Natasha.

She was dressed in Becky's costume, staring

into Becky's mirror, mouthing Becky's opening lines.

"You look wonderful," he said.

"I'm so frightened, Mark." She stood and went to him.

He put his arms around her. "You'll be great. The rehearsal was flawless, Natasha."

"But I didn't have thousands of eyes staring at me, did I? I will tonight."

"It's a full house according to Cyndy," he said.

Natasha gulped.

"And they'll all love you," he added. "My mother, especially."

"Has she arrived?" asked Natasha.

"Yes, I sent Cyndy out to scout … and Dad sent a note back with her." He reached into his pocket. "And he sent this one for you."

She read it and giggled. "What a flatterer!"

"What's it say?" he smiled.

She popped the note into her make-up box. "Let's just say he wishes me all the luck in the world."

"He really likes you," said Mark.

Natasha suddenly looked concerned. "I just hope I don't let him down."

Cyndy knocked and put her head round the door, announcing with a grin, "This is your five minute call, Ladies and Gentlemen."

"Thanks, Cyndy," said Natasha and Mark together.

She entered the room and kissed Natasha on the cheek. "Good luck, Natasha," she said. "You were brilliant in rehearsal. Break a leg!" She turned to Mark. "You don't need good luck," she said. "You're always brilliant."

As Cyndy left, Mark began to follow her.

"I'm going down to the wings," he said to Natasha. "Are you coming? Or do you want to wait for the final call?"

"I'll be down in a minute," she replied.

He left.

Natasha crossed to the full-length mirror, examining her costume and her make-up. She was determined to give the performance of a lifetime. She wanted to please Mark's father. She wanted Sam Coy and Bill Grant to learn how successful she'd been. She wanted to show Mark's mother what she was made of. But most of all she wanted Mark to be proud of her. That was the uppermost thought in her mind.

Cyndy rapped on the door again and entered.

"I'm just about to do the Beginners call," she said, "but this note was passed backstage, so I thought I'd better get this to you first."

"Thanks, Cyndy."

Natasha took the note … and Cyndy left the room and returned to the prompt-corner.

She didn't recognize the handwriting. She opened it.

"G'day!" it read. "Hobbled to Bournemouth on crutches to see how Mark was doing. And now I hear you're on with him tonight. What a gas! I'm with you all the way, babe. Lots o' love to you and Mark. Ashley."

"Beginners on stage, please," announced Cyndy.

*   *   *

The audience roared their approval after every musical number, helping Natasha's confidence to grow and grow … and as she and Mark sailed through the love duet, the title song from *A Stranger Love*, there was a deathly hush. Mark delivered the final lines with such incredible passion … more passion than he'd ever done before. And the audience rose to its feet as one, applauding thunderously and screaming out for an encore.

In the wings Cyndy whispered to the stage manager, "Bit good, isn't he?"

The stage manager laughed. "And she's not bad, either."

Relieved to reach her final speech, Natasha gave it everything she'd got.

The speech led to *A Stranger Love*'s reprise, bringing the audience to its feet once again.

Natasha sang:

Aching hearts are breaking; caring
  For nothing around me, while I'm sharing
A stranger's love.

Mark sang:

And though you mean the world to me;
  To the world there could never be
A stranger love.

And Jonathan held Sarah tightly in his arms.

JONATHAN: I love you, Sarah.

SARAH: And I love you.

THEY KISSED.

THE CURTAIN FELL.

The audience screamed and clapped and stamped.

Mark grinned. "Curtain call! Make-up off! And then let's face the in-laws!"

Natasha laughed.

"I've got something very important to tell my father," he added seriously.

"Oh?"

"I'm staying with the show, Natasha," he said. "As an understudy ... dogsbody ... chief bottle-washer. Who cares? I'll do anything they ask me ... as long as we're together."

"Oh, Mark!"

He held her tightly in his arms.

MARK: I love you, Natasha.

NATASHA: And I love you.

Point R♥mance

Caroline B. Cooney

The lives, loves and hopes of five young girls appear in this dazzling mini series:

Anne – coming to terms with a terrible secret that has changed her whole life.

Kip – everyone's best friend, but no one's dream date . . . why can't she find the right guy?

Molly – out for revenge against the four girls she has always been jealous of . . .

Emily – whose secure and happy life is about to be threatened by disaster.

Beth Rose – dreaming of love but wondering if it will ever become a reality.

Follow the five through their last years of high school, in four brilliant titles: *Saturday Night, Last Dance, New Year's Eve,* and *Summer Nights*

Point R♥mance

If you like Point Horror, you'll love Point Romance!

Anyone can hear the language of love.

**Are you burning with passion, and aching with desire?
Then these are the books for you! Point Romance brings
you passion, romance, heartache . . . and *love*.**

Point R♥mance

Look out for this heartwarming Point Romance
mini series:

First Comes Love

by Jennifer Baker

Can their happiness last?

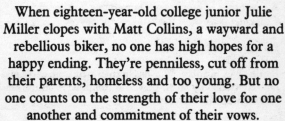

When eighteen-year-old college junior Julie
Miller elopes with Matt Collins, a wayward and
rebellious biker, no one has high hopes for a
happy ending. They're penniless, cut off from
their parents, homeless and too young. But no
one counts on the strength of their love for one
another and commitment of their vows.
Four novels, *To Have and To Hold, For Better
For Worse, In Sickness and in Health,* and *Till
Death Do Us Part*, follow Matt and Julie through
their first year of marriage.
Once the honeymoon is over, they have to deal
with the realities of life. Money worries,
tensions, jealousies, illness, accidents, and the
most heartbreaking decision of their lives.
Can their love survive?

Four novels to touch your heart . . .

POINT SF

Encounter worlds where men and women make hazardous voyages through space; where time travel is a reality and the fifth dimension a possibility; where the ultimate horror has already happened and mankind breaks through the barrier of technology . . .

The Obernewtyn Chronicles:
Book 1: Obernewtyn
Book 2: The Farseekers
Isobelle Carmody
A new breed of humans are born into a hostile world struggling back from the brink of apocalypse . . .

Random Factor
Jessica Palmer
Battle rages in space. War has been erased from earth and is now controlled by an all-powerful computer – until a random factor enters the system . . .

First Contact
Nigel Robinson
In 1992 mankind launched the search for extra-terrestial intelligence. Two hundred years later, someone responded . . .

Virus
Molly Brown
A mysterious virus is attacking the staff of an engineering plant . . . Who, or *what* is responsible?

Look out for:

Strange Orbit
Margaret Simpson

Scatterlings
Isobelle Carmody

Body Snatchers
Stan Nicholls

Read Point SF and enter a new dimension . . .

Point

Pointing the way forward

More compelling reading from top authors.

Flight 116 is Down
Caroline B. Cooney
Countdown to disaster . . .

Forbidden
Caroline B. Cooney
Theirs was a love that could never be . . .

Hostilities
Caroline Macdonald
In which the everyday throws shadows of another, more mysterious world . . .

Seventeenth Summer
K.M. Peyton
Patrick Pennington – mean, moody and out of control . . .

The Highest Form of Killing
Malcolm Rose
Death is in the very air . . .

Son of Pete Flude
Malcolm Rose
Being the son of an international rockstar is no easy trip . . .

Secret Lives
William Taylor
Two people drawn together by their mysterious pasts . . .

POINT FANTASY

Foiling the Dragon
Susan Price
What will become of Paul Welsh, pub poet,
when he meets a dragon – with a passion for
poetry, and an appetite for poets . . .

Dragonsbane
Patricia C. Wrede
Princess Cimorene discovers that living with a
dragon is not always easy, and there is a
serious threat at hand . . .

The Webbed Hand
Jenny Jones
Princess Maria is Soprafini's only hope
against the evil Prince Ferrian and his
monstrous Fireflies . . .

Look out for:
**Daine the Hunter:
Book 3: The Emperor Mage**
Tamora Price

Star Warriors
Peter Beere

**The "Renegades" Series
Book 3: The Return of the Wizard**
Jessica Palmer

Elf-King
Susan Price